"I'm pregnant."

Brett was glad he had his fist under his chin or his mouth would have dropped open.

"Please understand that I'm not telling you this because I want money or anything else from you. I'm not seeking a commitment of any kind."

"Wow," he finally said. "This is...pretty shocking news."

"I know," Summer said. "I'm only telling you because it seemed like I should. But you're..."

He leaned forward. "I'm what?"

She paused. "You're off the hook," she told him bluntly. "I want to raise the baby alone."

"I see." She wanted nothing to do with him. How could he argue with that? "If that's what you want," he finally said, attempting to sound unaffected.

The decision was made. Before Brett knew it, she was out of her seat and left without looking back.

This was...too much. She was having his baby. *His* baby.

And he'd just told her it was all right with him for her to raise that baby, *his* baby, alone.

What the hell had he been thinking?

Dear Reader,

As a writer, one of the things I enjoy most is discovering the hidden heart that beats inside each novel, the message in the book that I didn't even know myself until the words were on the page and the story complete.

In *Seducing Summer*, Summer and Brett's journey together is about many things—the sacrifices we make for the people we love, the control we attempt to maintain over our lives and, of course, what Temptation novel would be complete without a healthy dose of *passion?* Summer is a woman determined to keep control over her life in every way, but fortunately, Brett is a *very* persuasive guy, which results in a steamy connection between them from the moment they meet.

For me, though, I think the hidden heart of this book is *change*—how difficult it can be to make and accept major changes in our lives, and the realization that sometimes the changes we resist the most are the ones that make us happiest in the end.

If, by chance, you find your own hidden heart in this book, please let me know. You can visit me on the Web at http://www.toniblake.com or write to me at P.O. Box 17835, Covington, KY, 41017.

Sincerely,

Toni Blake

Books by Toni Blake

HARLEQUIN TEMPTATION
800—HOTBED HONEY

SEDUCING SUMMER
Toni Blake

Hope you enjoy!

Toni Blake

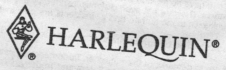

HARLEQUIN®

TORONTO • NEW YORK • LONDON
AMSTERDAM • PARIS • SYDNEY • HAMBURG
STOCKHOLM • ATHENS • TOKYO • MILAN • MADRID
PRAGUE • WARSAW • BUDAPEST • AUCKLAND

To Mom and Dad
for always being there,
and to Blair
for coming along when he did

ISBN 0-373-25925-5

SEDUCING SUMMER

Copyright © 2001 by Toni Herzog.

1

HE WASN'T THE MOST handsome man Summer Avery had ever seen, but there was something about him. An easy confidence that came without arrogance, a comfort with himself that was impossible not to see. He wore faded blue jeans and an open flannel shirt over a burgundy tee. From where Summer sat, his eyes looked dark—blue or brown, she couldn't tell—and that gave him a hint of allure. Or maybe more than a hint. Dark eyes spelled mystery, didn't they? The idea of mystery combined with a man so obviously comfortable in his own body made Summer begin to feel warm.

He bent over the pool table, a lock of dark hair falling waywardly over one eye. "Five ball in the corner," he said. The crack of the balls echoed across the room and the five dropped into the promised pocket. He lifted a triumphant gaze to his two opponents.

"Lucky shot, Ford," one of the guys said.

"*Luck,*" he replied with an arrogant grin, "has nothing to do with it. This is a sharply honed skill."

His pool buddies chuckled, and Summer found herself smiling, too.

Then she wondered just what the hell she was doing, staring at a guy across the bar, even listening in on his conversation. In fact, what was she doing here at all? This was all Tina's fault. And just where *was* Tina, any-

way? Summer silently vowed to kill her friend as soon
as she arrived.

This just figured. All of Summer's co-workers, including Tina, were always hounding her to get out more. So
what happened when she finally gave in and agreed to
go to happy hour with them? Suddenly none of them
were able to come. They had family dinners, hair ap-
pointments, grocery shopping—all of which Summer
could understand, but why had they pestered her to go,
only to leave her stranded? Tina was the only one who
hadn't canceled, and insisting they didn't need those
party poopers anyway, she'd refused to let Summer
back out. Tina had remained so enthusiastic that Summer had let her choose the place—a tiny watering hole in
suburbia—and now even *she* was standing Summer up.

"What can I get you, honey?" a gum-chewing, middle-aged waitress asked, breaking into Summer's
thoughts.

"A glass of chardonnay, please," she replied with a
forced smile.

If Tina didn't show up by the time Summer finished
her wine, she would feel totally justified in going home.
Besides, Summer knew what it meant when Tina and
everyone else insisted that she needed to get out more; it
really meant *you need to find a man*.

Yet at thirty, Summer was perhaps the only woman
she knew who was completely happy *not* having a man.
She had more important things to attend to, such as her
career, and if she'd learned anything at all in life, it was
that a family and commitments could only get in the
way.

"Here you go, sweetie," the waitress said when she
returned, lowering a stemmed glass before Summer. She

picked up the five-dollar bill Summer had laid on the table.

"Keep the change," Summer told her.

The way Summer saw it, a husband could do nothing but hold her back, make demands on her and keep her from doing her best in her career. She loved her job and had worked hard to get where she was, and nothing was more important to her.

Besides, not every soul had a mate. She was completely content to go home alone every night; her life was perfectly fulfilling as it stood.

And so what if Mr. Mysterious Eyes over there kept attracting her attention? She was single, not dead.

Every now and then she *tried* dating; it just didn't usually work out. Her mind flashed briefly to a long line of bad dates she'd been set up on. And even when the dates *weren't* bad, even when she'd fallen into an actual relationship here or there along the way, nothing earth-shattering had ever happened to her due to a man in her life.

So if that sexy guy caught her attention a little more than most, well, it was only because it had been a while since she'd gone out with anyone, and an even longer while since she'd been...*intimate* with a man.

His laughter rang out across the room then, even over the music that played, and she felt as if the sound taunted her. If she were a different sort of woman, maybe she'd saunter past him, to the ladies' room or the jukebox. Maybe she'd cast him a smile and try to start a conversation, flirt a little. But that wasn't her and it never had been—she'd never really learned *how* to flirt.

She took a long swallow of her wine, draining half the glass. Another sip or two like that and the glass would be empty and she'd be out of here. Soon she'd be home, curled up on her sofa in her favorite flannel pajamas with a good book, right where she belonged.

And Mr. Mysterious Eyes would be *here*, with his sharply honed skills and his ringing laughter, right where *he* belonged.

Some things could not be meshed.

"You forfeiting your shot or what?"

Summer looked at the pool table. The question had been directed at the attractive guy and she immediately saw why—*he was staring at her*. Their eyes met and held for the space of a heartbeat before she shifted her gaze to her wineglass.

"Considering that the losers buy the beer," she heard him say, "no way."

The moment was over, quick as that, and it was a relief, really. Because the last thing she'd expected was to find those arresting eyes turned on *her*. She took a deep breath just to make sure she still could. Then, feeling much more curious than seemed prudent, she let her glance drift cautiously back in his direction as he studied his next shot.

"Side pocket," he said, gesturing to his right. He pulled back his cue and sent the eight ball rolling neatly into the designated hole. "Beer's on you guys," he said with a grin.

Summer watched with her peripheral vision as Mr. Mysterious Eyes and his friends moved to the bar. She was glad the game of pool was over, glad the surreptitious glancing game had ended, as well.

She sighed and drummed her manicured fingernails on the table. Where was Tina? Two more minutes, Summer vowed silently. Two more minutes and if Tina didn't show, she was out of here. The relief she'd felt at the ending of the pool game had been ridiculously short-lived—mere seconds. And even with the men's backs to her, Summer still felt somehow conspicuous, like a headline that read Lonely Woman Sits In Bar Waiting To Get Lucky.

"Okay, I'm here. Don't kill me."

Summer looked up as Tina slid into the booth across from her, her shoulder-length auburn hair bouncing and her perky nose red from the cold.

Summer breathed a sigh of relief at her friend's arrival. "Thank goodness," she said. "I was beginning to think I had the wrong place or something."

"Nope, it's the right place," Tina said, "but traffic's bad, I couldn't find a place to park and it's snowing outside."

Only then did Summer notice the white snowflakes on the shoulders of Tina's trendy faux snakeskin jacket as she shrugged out of it. "Well, I can relate about the parking," Summer admitted. "I had to park three blocks away."

"I know you're not fond of going to bars by yourself," Tina said with an apologetic tilt of her head. Although Summer had been trying not to let her discomfort show, she supposed she'd failed. "So I'm really sorry I'm late. On top of the weather and the traffic, Henderson stopped me on the way out of the office with questions about spring purchasing. But I'm here now, so you can relax and we can have fun."

"Fun," Summer said, smiling. "Whoopee," she added, twirling her finger in the air.

Half an hour later, Tina had finished one gin and tonic and started another, and Summer was refusing a third glass of wine, since she had to drive and hoped to start home soon. She hated to spoil Tina's grand plan, but she was ready to go. Mr. Mysterious Eyes still sat at the bar with his friends, and Summer had the strange feeling that the sooner she got away from him, the better. Not that she'd been thinking about him this whole time. She hadn't. She just thought this happy-hour idea had been a silly waste of an evening. "Well," she began, preparing to break the news of her departure, "I think I'm going to—"

"Tina? Tina Conway?"

Where had that deep voice come from? And why did it sound so familiar? Summer lifted her eyes and held in her gasp as shock traveled the length of her body. It was him—Mr. Mysterious Eyes! And he was headed this way!

"Oh my God! Is that you, Brett?"

Tina was on her feet and embracing him before Summer could blink. Oh boy. This was *not* what she needed.

A moment ago she'd almost forgotten he existed.

Okay, maybe that was a lie, but a moment ago she *had* been ready to go home and forget about the guy.

And now...well, now she felt completely stuck in place at the table, her gaze glued helplessly to him.

"Brett Ford," Tina said when the hug finally ended, "meet my boss and friend, Summer Avery. Brett was my boyfriend's roommate in college," Tina added with a smile, "and he's also about the greatest guy on the earth. We haven't seen each other in—what—nine or ten years?"

Brett laughed. "More like eleven by my count. I was two years ahead of Danny, remember?"

"Oh," Tina said, "that's right."

Brett held out his hand to Summer and she found herself daring to look up into eyes that transfixed her, and suddenly weren't so mysterious, but just a shade lighter than midnight blue. Nope, this was really *not* what she needed. Her stomach did a somersault as she reached tentatively for his hand.

SHE WAS PERHAPS the most beautiful woman Brett Ford had ever seen, but there was something about her. A certain tenseness, a definite discomfort with her surroundings. Her pale green eyes were lovely, yet they lacked...softness. He'd almost thought that aloof attitude was changing during his game of pool when, from the corner of his eye, he'd seen her smiling at his silly remark. But the smile had disappeared almost as quickly as it had come, like heat lightning on a summer night.

She wore a serious yet stylish business suit—the olive shade helped to bring out the color of her eyes—and her short blond hair fell in careful and precise-looking waves to frame her face. She was perfect. Maybe a little *too* perfect. Except for that brief hint of light he'd seen in her eyes from across the room, she'd kept her gaze down, her face expressionless. Yes, she was a beautiful woman, but Brett got the idea she meant to warn people away.

Well, if that was her plan, it'd been working. Had she revealed even the tiniest hint of interest earlier, he might have come over, bought her a drink, sat and talked with her. But she'd been sending out all the signals that said, *Go away.* Brett wasn't stupid; he'd planned to heed them. Only now all that had changed. Tina was introducing him to Summer Avery, whose name reminded him of a breeze, and he was more than a little curious to see her response.

She shook his hand with a short, quick grasp he suspected she used when doing business, then pulled back her long, tapered fingers before he even got to enjoy touching them.

"You and Danny didn't get married or anything, did you?" he asked Tina before smiling into Summer Avery's misty, cool eyes again.

Tina's friendly laugh met his ears. "Are you kidding? We broke up the day after graduation and I haven't seen him since. How about you and Joni?"

"No," he said, as Tina pulled him down beside her in the booth. "We parted ways about a year after college. I came home, got a job with Foster-Hardin, and I've been here ever since."

"Oh yeah," Tina said, "I forgot you grew up in Cincinnati, too."

He nodded. "My mom was thrilled when I came home to get a job, and it *is* nice to be close to my family. I have nieces and a nephew now, and I wouldn't want to miss out on all that. So," he said, grinning, "what are *you* doing?"

"I work at Stafford's as the assistant to the senior buyer," Tina proudly replied. Brett smiled inwardly. Tina had been in the accounting program at Ohio State, but he remembered thinking she had more of a head for fashion.

The opening gave him a chance to look back at her friend, another opportunity to break down that wall of hers. "Would that make you the senior buyer then?"

Summer Avery nodded shortly, but gave no details. "And...Foster-Hardin?" she asked. "That's...?"

"An architectural firm downtown," he replied. "We design mostly office buildings and complexes. Business environments."

She nodded again, but Brett didn't miss the small flash of respect in her eyes. She obviously hadn't expected him to be that far up in the occupational food chain. And why the hell he cared what she thought of him he didn't know. Hadn't he already decided to read this lady's warning signals? Still, it was hard not to want to find out more about her, not to want to get a little closer and uncover what made her so aloof. Damn, she really *was* beautiful. Much more so when she let her eyes sparkle—something he'd seen twice now, even if only fleetingly. How could he not want to find a way to make it happen again?

"Can I get you a drink?" he asked, motioning to the empty wineglass before her.

"No, thank you," she said staidly.

A low, trilling noise promptly interrupted Brett's sense of rejection, and he looked to see Tina digging a cell phone from her purse.

"Hello," she answered. "Mmm-hmm...okay. No, it's no problem, Mom...really." Then she snapped the phone shut and released a heavy sigh.

"Something wrong?" Brett asked.

"I'm afraid I have to leave," she said. "My mother is sick."

"Nothing serious, is it?" Summer asked.

Tina shook her head. "Just flu symptoms. But she's getting older and she's alone now, and she asked me to come over. I'll go make her some soup, maybe watch TV with her for a while."

Tina shoved her phone back in her purse, and Brett let her out of the booth and helped her on with her jacket. "Need me to walk you to your car?"

She smiled appreciatively. "That's sweet of you, Brett, but I'll be fine." Then she switched her gaze to her boss. "And I'm really sorry to have to cut this short, Summer."

"Don't worry about it. I know how it is. Tell your mom I hope she feels better." Still, Brett thought Summer looked disconcerted even as she gave Tina an understanding smile.

"Thanks, Summer. I'll see you tomorrow. And it was great bumping into you, Brett." Turning, Tina headed across the bar and out the door, and Summer and Brett were left alone.

"Well..." he said, with a hopeful glance in her direction. He hated to see Tina leave so soon, but maybe this would give him a chance to make Summer Avery's eyes sparkle again.

"Well..." she returned, and she even offered him the hint of a smile before stopping him in his tracks with, "I really should go, too."

"You should? I mean, already?"

"Yes," she said, reaching beside her for her purse. "I have to work tomorrow and Tina says it's snowing out, so I should drive home before the roads get bad, and—"

"Have one drink with me."

Summer caught her breath. Oh no, he was flirting with her. She hadn't exactly anticipated this. Or maybe she had. Maybe that's why she was in such a hurry to leave. The way he looked at her, time and again...it weakened her in a way she'd never encountered and didn't think she liked. If there was one thing she couldn't afford, it was weakness.

"But I really—"

"Come on," he pleaded, a boyish expression on his face. "Give a guy a break."

She couldn't help smiling at him, and he returned it. Yet even as appealing as she found his somewhat crooked grin, she hated letting him think he'd worn her down that easily, so she said, "I'll stay for a few minutes, but I don't want a drink, since I have to drive."

"Fair enough," he said. "How about a game of pool instead?"

She released a laugh before she could hold it in. "Me? Pool? I don't think so. Especially against a man with such sharply honed skills."

His grin widened with recognition that made her want to bury her head. She'd just given herself away. "I overheard you before," she admitted.

"That's okay," he said. "I knew you did. I saw you smile."

She felt the blush climb her cheeks, yet she wasn't truly embarrassed. In fact, she noticed right away that it was hard to *get* embarrassed with Brett Ford—he never gave you the impression that you *should* be.

"Come on," he said, rising from the seat across from her and holding out one hand. "Let's play."

The words made her heart beat a little faster. "But I don't know how—"

"I'll teach you."

And as if a force greater than herself was taking over, she felt her hand being lifted into the warmth of his, her body gliding from the booth and across the wooden floor to the pool table. Never before in her life had she played pool. Never before had she wanted to. If anyone had told her an hour ago that she'd have accepted such an invitation, she'd have said that person was crazy. Now it seemed *she* was the crazy one.

"Wow," she mused, looking around, "it's quiet in here all of a sudden." While music still played, there was no crowd. A little while ago, at least twenty people had milled about the small suburban bar. Now she saw no one else but the two guys Brett had been playing pool with, and even they were putting on their coats.

"See ya, buddy," one of them said with a wave.

"Later, guys," Brett replied. Then he turned to Summer, "Yeah, except for the weekends, Dunbar's is an after work sort of place. Seven o'clock comes and most people have to clear out, go home to be with their families, that kind of thing."

"Except for you," she said.

"And except for you. Which makes me a lucky guy."

Summer's heartbeat quickened when he looked at her. He was flirting again. Or maybe he had been the whole time. Maybe she'd actually been flirting, too. How on earth had *that* happened?

"Ready to play?" he asked, pulling two cues from the rack on the wall. She couldn't keep from associating his words with sexual meaning, and the question almost paralyzed her. But that didn't keep her entire body from tingling when he wrapped both arms around her from behind and said, "Here's how you hold the pool cue."

He pressed his body softly against hers and brought his arms down on either side. A tender ache lodged in the small of Summer's back as he clasped her hands and wrapped them around the cue. "Now," he whispered, "aim for the ball in front."

How could she concentrate on playing pool when all she could think about were the strong, warm fingers that had just left hers? The sturdy male body that had just pulled away? Talk about feeling weak. Yet this feeling assaulting her now...well, it was a sensation she found hard to hate.

Finally, she drew back the cue and gave it her best. The white ball rolled toward the triangle of colored ones, colliding with them gently. They barely scattered, but it was enough to send one plunking into a corner pocket. She looked up to find Brett shaking his head with a grin.

"Are you sure you aren't conning me? Sure you haven't played this game before?"

No, this was definitely one game she hadn't played before, but she wasn't even thinking about pool. Instead she equated the game to the flash of his smile, the sensual light in his eyes. Of all the men she'd ever dated, she'd never been attracted to one this strongly, and she had no idea of her next move.

"Still your shot," he said, as if reading her thoughts. When she hesitated, he moved around the pool table behind her and whispered in her ear, telling her which ball to aim for, encouraging her to take her time. But all she could think about was the low sound of his voice and the warmth of his breath on her neck. How on earth could she be expected to concentrate with all this sensual distraction?

Summer's early luck didn't hold. By the time the game ended, she'd only taken four shots. Still, each one had required his help, his body, his hands—that intimate heat of human connection. She felt as if they'd shared much more than a few minutes of billiards. Her chest tightened as she wondered what would happen next.

After he sank the last ball, though, he simply looked up at her and smiled. "Thanks for playing," he said, then turned to put away his cue.

A surprising feeling of disappointment bit into Summer's spine. This was it? He was releasing her, sending her home?

But hadn't that been her aim from the beginning? Why did her stomach seem to plummet at what she took for a simple dismissal?

Apparently, she'd been wrong, and a game of pool was really all they'd shared. Silly of her to read anything more into it. Now it was time to ignore that nagging little pain inside and start acting like herself—she had dignity to maintain, after all. "You're welcome," she said, lowering her eyes so he wouldn't see any emotion that might be leaking free without her permission. Then she moved back across the floor to the booth, where she reached for her coat.

"Grab a bite to eat with me before you go?" he asked from behind.

It was as if he'd just lifted an anvil from her chest. She turned to look at him. "Um, where?"

"They have nachos and wings here," he said with a shrug. "We could split an order of each."

Nachos and wings. Not her usual fare. But whether she liked it or not, this night was becoming something more than usual, and Summer couldn't have been happier if he'd offered her champagne and caviar.

AN HOUR AND TWO PLATES of greasy food later, Brett had seen her eyes sparkle more times than he'd originally thought possible. He'd misjudged Summer Avery. She wasn't so cold, nor so tough. Her outer shell had been cracked and broken away with just a few smiles, some laughter and a tender touch or two.

It was those tender touches that had him in trouble now. Holding her during their game of pool had been deliberate, and pleasurable, and easy enough to slide by her as necessary to the teaching process. But now their nachos were gone and their glasses were empty, and he had a feeling Summer was about to drop the it's-time-for-me-to-leave bomb on him when he was more than ready to start touching her again.

"Another soda?" he asked, in hopes of delaying the inevitable.

She shook her head and wiped a napkin across her

mouth—the mouth he wanted to touch with his fingers, the mouth he had the overpowering urge to kiss.

"I should go," she said, checking her watch.

Boom. "What time is it?" he asked.

"After nine."

"Past your bedtime?" He punctuated the question with a grin.

"Something like that," she said, her eyes guarded.

"Don't suppose I could talk you into another game of pool?"

Was he crazy, or did she actually look tempted? "Um...no," she said anyway. "I really should get home. I have an eight o'clock meeting in the morning."

He gave a short nod. Time for plan two. "Then you'll at least give me your number, won't you?"

Summer swallowed. For the past hour and a half, she'd felt gloriously drunk, but she hadn't even been drinking. It was the affect Brett Ford had on her. Now his request sobered her. He wanted this flirtation to go on. For another night. Maybe for lots of other nights. It would be easy to say yes, to whip out a pen and scrawl her number across a napkin and tuck it into the pocket of his shirt. After all, hadn't Tina said he was the greatest guy ever? Since Tina knew him, Summer didn't even have to worry about him being an ax murderer or anything.

But maybe there was a reason Summer had only ever dated guys she thought of as being "average," guys who didn't, *couldn't*, excite her the way Brett Ford did. She didn't want to get attached to anyone because she didn't want to give up the control of her life that she'd waited so long to regain. And this drunken giddiness she felt for him, this melting weakness that had come over her from the first moment their eyes met...Summer couldn't take any more of that. There was too much risk, too many complications she didn't need. She was an independent woman and she intended to keep it that way.

"Brett, I'm afraid I can't," she finally said, thinking she sounded surprisingly sure.

"Can't?" he repeated, raising his eyebrows. Then he gave her a playful smile, the kind that reminded her all too well of why she was refusing him—he melted her heart with far too much ease. "Don't tell me you've been cheating on me, Summer. Please say I'm the only one."

Oh drat, she smiled. But she let it fade as she tried to think how to explain. "The thing is...I'm a busy woman. It's...my job. I was just recently promoted to senior buyer and it's a huge responsibility that takes up all my time."

"You're here tonight."

"A rare reprieve. At Tina's insistence."

He nodded, looking disappointed, but not surprised. It made her feel sad and strangely predictable, as if he were offering her a wonderful gift and she just wouldn't open it. Yet that didn't change things. "I don't really have time for—"

He held up a hand. "Stop. You don't have to go on. I understand."

This caught her off guard. "You do?"

"Sure," he said with the same easy confidence that had initially drawn her to him. "A woman only has to turn me down four or five times before I take the hint," he laughed. "But thanks for sharing the wings and nachos with me. And I'm sorry you won't let me see you again, but it was a nice night, huh?"

A tremor rippled through her. A nice night? More than he could possibly know. She nodded, suddenly wishing he would beg and plead with her, explain to her all the reasons she shouldn't say no, tell her how wonderful it could all be.

But it's best this way, she scolded herself. *It really is.*

"Where are you parked?" Brett asked as he helped slide her coat onto her shoulders.

She pointed. "A few blocks that way."

"Great," he said easily. "I happen to *live* a few blocks that way. I'll walk you." Then he glanced out a window, where snow still fell in large flakes past the glow of streetlamps. "Bundle up," he said, raising the collar of the leather jacket he'd just put on. "The bank sign across the street says it's only eighteen degrees." He drew a pair of black leather gloves from his pocket.

Summer buttoned her tailored wool coat and wrapped her scarf around her neck as he waited.

"Ready?" he asked from near the door.

"Ready," she said, hoisting her purse strap onto her shoulder and crossing the room toward him.

Yet when she reached him, he tilted his head and chided her with his eyes. "Wait a minute. You're not ready." He peered at her hands. "No gloves?"

"I forgot them at work."

He cast her a reproving look. "Summer, it's eighteen degrees out there."

"I know, but I forgot them. It's no big deal."

He gave his head a slight shake, still in that remonstrative way. "Here," he said, taking off his right glove. "Put this on."

"What?"

"Just trust me."

As they stepped out onto the sidewalk, now covered with snow, Summer did as he asked, sliding her right hand into his big warm glove. Then he took her left arm, looping it through his, and gently pulled her bare hand into the pocket of his coat, letting his hand stay inside, too, covering hers. Summer caught her breath and felt a tingle between her thighs. How could it be only eighteen degrees out here when her entire body was overcome with heat?

"Warm?" he asked.

"Mmm," she said, thinking that it was *more* than warm, the intimate gesture unexpected and thrilling.

"Good."

They walked, silent, as the snow falling around them transformed the neighborhood into a wintry wonderland. Funny, she'd have thought she'd wanted to use these last few minutes with him to talk more, but she didn't regret their quietness—it seemed fitting, and even romantic, to share the snowfall. Somewhere during the walk, their fingers became interlocked inside his coat pocket and the heat from their hands radiated throughout Summer's body.

"Well, here's my car," she said as they approached a residential street corner. Reaching the spot left her feeling half relieved and half filled with sorrow.

"And there's my place," he said, pointing to a large, beige frame house with German features, like much of Cincinnati's older architecture. "Well, actually, I just live on the top floor," he amended. "I rent from Mrs. Greenbaum downstairs."

Summer regretfully pulled her hand from his pocket, and his warmth, and began fishing in her purse for her keys. She suddenly felt awkward, anxious to get away. She feared that if she didn't depart soon, she'd be tempted to retract her refusal to see him again.

"Lucky for you that you parked here," he said.

She couldn't help smiling up at him, even as her body burned with the need to escape. "Why's that?"

"Well," he said, "this way you can get warmed up inside the car while I scrape the snow and frost off your windows."

Something fluttered a bit in Summer's heart at the sweet offer, yet she let herself gaze at him only briefly. She then led him around to the driver's side, got in and found her scraper under the seat. "Thank you," she said, handing it up to him.

"My pleasure," he replied. He closed the door, shutting her inside, and Summer eased the key into the ignition, her mind racing with conflicting thoughts. *It's good that I'm getting out of here and going home, but it would have been nice to feel more of his warmth.*

Ah, but she shouldn't wish for such things. She should just be glad he'd taken no for an answer and been so gentlemanly about it, too.

Twisting the key, she heard the engine turn over, but it didn't quite rumble to life. A little dart of panic spiraled down Summer's spine; her car *always* started on the first try. Pressing her foot to the gas pedal, she tried again, only to hear that same grating sound.

A few unsuccessful tries later, as she was beginning to feel desperate, her car door opened. Beneath the glow of streetlights, Brett's friendly face beamed down on her, his dark hair sprinkled with snow. "Looks like car trouble," he said, his voice laced with sympathy.

She nodded, beginning to feel a little helpless and as if fate were conspiring against her where this man was concerned.

"Probably just dead from the cold," he said. "This corner tends to catch a harsh wind in the wintertime that makes things freeze up pretty fast. I wish I could tell you I have a set of jumper cables," he concluded with a commiserating tilt of his head, "but I don't."

Summer let her eyes shut in despair for a second before opening them to say, "Me, neither."

"Not very responsible of us, is it?" he asked with a small, consoling smile.

"No, I suppose not," she said, but she turned her head to peer out the windshield he'd begun to clear, because looking at him again was making her *want* him again, that quickly.

"I'd call Triple A for you, but I just let my membership expire," he said.

"*Triple A!*" she exclaimed, as if she'd just discovered a cure for a rare disease. "I have Triple A!" She'd forgotten about it entirely, because she'd never had a reason to actually use it before.

Brett smiled down on her, which made her realize she was staring at him again, drat it all. "Great," he said, "problem solved. Come on inside and we'll give them a call."

Inside? Summer thought. *His house?* It only made sense that she would go inside now, of course, yet a frisson of uncertainty—or was that excitement?—raced through Summer's veins. Every time she thought the night was ending, it went on. It had been hard enough to refuse giving him her number, hard enough to stick to her decision as they'd walked together, but this made everything immensely more difficult.

She knew she should find some way to refuse before she was tempted to do anything stupid, knew she should just tell him she'd find a phone booth or walk back to the bar and wait there. It would sound preposterous, though, especially with his house right here and the bar three blocks away, and her with no gloves on top of it all. In fact, it would seem downright irrational.

"Good idea," she finally said, stepping out of the car and back into the snowy street.

Moments later, they climbed the stairs to the second floor entrance of Brett's apartment. Once inside, he turned on the lights and told her to take off her coat.

"Hot chocolate?" he asked, shrugging free of his jacket and flannel shirt, tossing them both on a coat rack by the door.

But she hadn't planned on staying even *that* long. "You don't have to—"

"Oh, come on," he said, cutting off her protest. "I have all these little packets of cocoa my mother gives me, and never any reason to use them. Indulge me."

Summer sighed, then conceded. She was making too much of this, being too worrisome. It was only hot chocolate. "Oh, all right," she said. "I suppose it *would* be nice."

"Warm you up for the drive home," he told her. He moved about the small kitchen area, putting the cocoa mix and water into mugs and putting the mugs into the microwave.

Summer found her Triple A card in her purse and quickly made the call, only to get some distressing news. She hung up the phone with a frown.

"What's wrong?" Brett asked.

Summer sighed as she turned to face him. "It's going to be at least an hour," she said, her stomach tight with dismay. "Apparently I'm not the only one with a dead battery tonight."

But Brett only smiled. "Not a problem. I'm just glad you were with me when this happened, so you have someplace warm to wait."

The ding of the microwave interrupted their conversation, and Brett pulled out two steaming mugs of hot chocolate. Meanwhile, Summer started looking around the apartment, which she found small and simple, but rich with character. "Great woodwork," she said of the wide doorway that led from the open kitchen-living area into the next room, the intricately carved trim stained cherry.

"Thanks," he said, glancing up. "I did it myself."

Summer couldn't help being impressed. Apparently he was more than just an architect; he was a hands-on kind of guy, too. A ripple ran through her. Why had she had to think that—*a hands-on guy?*

"That was originally just a single doorway," he said, "but I widened it and put on the double doors leading to the bedroom. I opened up the ceiling in there, too, to make it a cathedral. And I put in this kitchen."

For Summer, being impressed got closer to being astounded. "Wow, your landlady must love you."

He responded with the same crooked grin she recalled from earlier. "Actually, we made a deal—I didn't pay rent for the first few months in exchange for the improvements. Now, if I ever move out, she can keep renting the place. She's older, so it's an important source of income for her."

Summer joined him at the small kitchen table then, where they sat across from each other, their knees touching lightly underneath. She hated herself for not shifting her knees away, but somehow she just couldn't. She felt strange and disconnected from her normal self, as if this situation was gradually beginning to spin out of control. She couldn't believe she had to last another whole hour with him.

Maybe she'd been too quick to decide that going back to the bar would have been unreasonable, or that drinking hot chocolate with him was no big deal. After all, despite the cold temperatures outside, at the moment she really didn't need to be any warmer than she already was.

"So, Summer Avery," he said softly, blowing on his cocoa, then shifting his gaze to hers. "You still don't think you could work me into your schedule?"

Summer felt herself blush at the question. After all, their knees were touching and they both knew it, and still she was going to tell him no. How much sense did that make? Well, unfortunately, it made plenty to her. Nonetheless, her breath caught when she started to speak. "It's not that I wouldn't like to, Brett...."

He glanced down, then took a careful sip from his cup. "I know, I know," he said. "Your job is your life or something like that."

"Yes," she replied, biting her lip, then taking a quick drink of hot chocolate and letting the warmth flood her. She had to get her control back here; she couldn't let this situation weaken her resolve. "My job is extremely important to me. I've had to work very hard and wait a long time to get where I am."

"I can respect that," he said, "but a job isn't everything, Summer."

She took a deep breath. "To me, it is." She glanced down into her mug, a silent signal that she didn't want to continue the conversation.

He must have gotten the message, because he didn't reply. But beneath the table, their knees still touched, and he shifted ever so slightly, just enough to let one of hers slide between his, where he gently took it captive.

Summer pulled in her breath. Their gazes met across the table. She could clearly read the desire written in his eyes. Oh God, what secrets might her own be telling?

Control, control, she whispered inside. The one-word

mantra would be the only thing to save her. If only she could hear it, heed it. *Control.*

"Thanks for the hot chocolate," she said, rising suddenly from the table, "but I'm sure the Triple A guys are on their way by now, so I should probably go outside and wait for them."

"It's eighteen degrees outside, Summer," he reminded her, "and it's only been a few minutes."

"Yes, well," she said quickly, "they told me to be outside by my car so they could find it."

He rose from his seat as well—not nearly as hurriedly as she had—and offered a small but accepting smile. "You really don't want to be here, do you?"

The question jarred her; she hadn't expected him to be so up front. Yet she supposed she owed him the same honesty, so she tried to give it. "Let's just say…it seems like a bad idea." Without hesitation, she retrieved her coat from the coat tree and briskly slid it on. *Control.* If only she could get out that door without losing it.

She was surprised to find Brett in front of her then, pulling the collar of her coat up around her neck, holding tight to her lapels. Oh God, his face was suddenly close, *too* close. She thought she might faint. She wanted to kiss him. *Control,* she whispered, but it was nowhere to be found.

"Surely you'll let me kiss you good-night," he breathed.

She opened her mouth to protest, but nothing came out.

Then she began to tremble and he leaned near, and as her lips parted involuntarily, he brushed the lightest of all possible kisses across them. "Oh…" she murmured as the blood in her veins turned to lava.

"More?" he whispered.

She looked into his eyes and released a heavy breath that they both knew meant yes. Any lingering thoughts of control fled her mind.

Brett's lips met hers in a slow, deep kiss that nearly turned Summer inside out. He still held on to her coat, but soon released it, taking her face in his hands and making Summer feel as if she were the only thing that existed in his world. She pressed her palms against his chest, thinking how warm and sturdy he felt. When his tongue slipped past her lips, she responded instinctually, letting it find hers, letting them taste each other in a slow, sexy rhythm that would have made her feel unsteady if his hold on her hadn't been so strong.

Finally, he drew his hands down to her shoulders, where he pushed her coat off, letting it fall to her elbows, and he kept kissing her—warm, deep, overpowering.

Next he reached down to undo the gold button that held her suit jacket closed and smoothly slid that from her shoulders, as well. He still kissed her, and her mouth trembled beneath his, wanting more.

Everything grew hazy when she sensed his fingers working at her blouse. One button, then another. And the kissing, the sweet, hot kissing. Oh God, it was all moving so fast, like a runaway train. She'd lost control completely. At the moment, she hardly knew the meaning of the word.

Brett's mouth finally left her lips and dropped to her neck, which arched for him involuntarily. Each moist kiss sent a bolt of electricity rushing through her, and it was all she could do not to whimper.

When he'd unbuttoned her blouse to her waist, Brett stopped and drew back to look at her. Blue eyes as dark as the night penetrated her very soul, and every part of her body quaked. He was asking her with his gaze, *Do we stop or do we go on?*

As with someone dying, Summer's life flashed before her when she peered into Brett's deep, wanting eyes. She'd never had this before. This passion, this fire, this *need* that coursed through her now. *Never.* And control? It was nothing but a meaningless word.

She pulled her hands from his chest and let them drop to her sides, sending her coat, jacket and blouse falling to the floor in a heap.

She'd never had this before, but she would have it tonight.

"Yes," she whispered. "Yes."

Brett's eyes glazed with anticipation before he scooped her into his arms and carried her through the wide doorway to his bedroom, lit only by a dim swath of light that streamed from the kitchen. He lowered her to a wrought-iron bed, where a soft blanket lay beneath her and a cool pillow cradled her head.

Bending over her, he slid his strong hands to the white lace cups of her bra. He gently kneaded her and she leaned back her head, listening to the heated sounds of her own breath. She could scarcely believe this was happening, but his touch felt too perfect to resist.

He lowered soft kisses to the exposed skin at the tops of her breasts, and she wanted more, yet he retreated, kneeling next to her on the bed. Reaching down, he deftly removed both of her shoes, letting them fall to the carpet below. She thought he would finish undressing her then, and she began to have thoughts of undressing him, too, when he lowered a soft kiss to her toes, making her gasp.

The nylon of her panty hose did nothing to dull the sensations as Brett's mouth slowly climbed her calf with tender, skimming kisses that made her shiver. When he lifted her leg and kissed the back of her knee, she moaned, and when he began the long, slow ascent up her inner thigh, Summer began to tremble until she thought she would come apart at the seams. Higher he moved his caressing mouth, pushing her skirt up with his hands as he went until his kisses lingered so close to the juncture of her thighs that she wanted to scream.

When he pulled back, she *did* scream—just a short, little, frustrated cry—but Brett didn't respond, and that somehow added to her excitement. She knew then that it was all by design, that he meant to push her to the edge and back again, that he meant to drive her wild. This was no ordinary lovemaking.

He reached beneath her skirt and found the top edge of her panty hose, rolling them down her legs and off in one long, fluid motion. "Lift up," he whispered, then stretched his arms around to unzip her skirt, pulling it off, as well.

After that, his hands and mouth moved over her calves and thighs, hips and tummy, arms and breasts, shoulders and neck, all in a wondrous rhapsody of sensuality that made Summer forget everything but this man and what he was doing to her body.

When he finally undid the front clasp of her bra and took her bare breasts into his hands, Summer sighed with joy. He stroked his thumbs over her beaded nipples, and she moaned as ripples of pleasure vibrated through her.

Feeling aggressive, she locked her legs around his back and began to pull at his T-shirt, wanting it off of him. He drew it over his head and flung it aside, and she kneaded his strong chest until he finally released his own growl of pleasure. He moved against her panties, and even through his jeans, she could feel how hard he was.

She bit her lip before commanding him, "Take them off."

He rose and did as she asked, discarding his jeans on the floor. But instead of climbing back on top of her, he rolled to his side and said, "Now your turn. Take off your panties."

Summer hooked her thumbs into the white silk at her hips, lifted her bottom from the bed, pushed her panties to her ankles and then tossed them away.

"Your turn again," she whispered heatedly. "Take off your underwear."

He did, and Summer's breath caught in her throat when she saw him. Even in the dim lighting, there was no mistaking how ready he was for her, and her entire body pulsed with desire. When she finally raised her eyes to his in the semidarkness, the same crooked grin she was coming to know painted his face with sensual amusement—he'd seen her looking.

Then, without warning, he pushed her to her back, gently pinning her arms above her. He licked and suckled her breasts as he slid one hand between her legs, making her whimper at the touch. "You're so wet," he breathed.

She didn't answer, *couldn't* answer. He'd taken her by storm.

"I'll make you wetter," he whispered, and Summer gasped at the promise. Parting her legs, he moved down her body and began stroking her with his tongue, long, lush strokes that made her cry out and hold on tightly to the wrought-iron bed frame above her head. Oh, this was really happening! The reality of it was still hard for her to fathom, but then she began to get lost in it, lose touch with space and time and reality, lose touch with everything but sensation.

Soon he rose up from her, teasing her again, leaving her to suffer his abandonment, but she soon realized he'd only stopped to reach into a drawer on a bedside table. She heard the rip and resisted the urge to tell him to hurry. Clenching her teeth, she gripped the bed above her, thinking, *Please, please.*

Then he was there, pushing himself into her—deep, deeper—forcing a guttural moan from the depths of her soul as he entered. He was groaning, too, whispering to her again, his breath warm in her ear as he said, "You're so tight." She resisted another urge, this one to tell him that it had been a while. He didn't need to know that— she didn't need to share it. She only wanted him to enjoy her as much as she was enjoying him.

He moved inside her, all the while kissing her lips, neck, breasts. She breathed heavily beneath him, unashamed of the sounds, unashamed of how exquisite she felt and how lost she was to him.

"I want you on top of me," he said suddenly, rolling to his back and lifting her to straddle him all in one incredible movement that almost took Summer's breath. It seemed that he was even deeper inside her then, deeper than she could have imagined. Nothing in her life had ever made her feel more excited to the very tips of her fingers and toes than she was in this moment. He'd made love to her, and now he wanted *her* to make love to *him*.

Looking into his eyes, she trembled anew. He reached for her breasts, pushing them up, grazing the taut nipples with the tips of his thumbs as she slowly began to move on him.

As he released a breath beneath her, her body took

over, leading her in tiny orbits over and around his hardness inside her. A familiar energy grew deep within her womb—familiar, yet new and different. She knew what it was like to come with a man, but she already knew that coming with *this* man would be unlike anything she'd ever known.

She pressed her hands to his chest as she moved on him, and gazed into the heated eyes that watched her. She abandoned her body to that heat, to the driving need, and let it take over, let it deliver her there. "Oh," she whispered, getting close.

He moaned, and the sound connected with her soul and pushed her over the edge. A thousand waves of light cascaded over her, electricity pulsing through her fingers and toes. She let her head fall back in ecstasy, let it all happen to her, let him watch what he'd done to her.

Soon it was happening for him, too. He was whispering her name as he drove up into her, high and deep, emptying himself in her body and then pulling her down, warm and snug against his chest, bestowing a single soft kiss to her forehead.

A long, languid moment later, Summer surprised herself by releasing a tiny bit of laughter. He shifted beneath her and she lifted her head to meet sated blue eyes. "What?" he whispered.

"I was just wondering…is this another of your sharply honed skills?"

The small, playful smile came with only a hint of arrogance. "As a matter of fact, it is."

AT THE LOSS OF HIS WARMTH, Summer realized he'd pulled away from her. "Where are you going?"

Her eyes focused in the dim light and she saw that

he'd put his jeans back on. He cast her a soft grin. "I'm gonna go see if the Triple A guys are here yet."

Her car. She'd totally forgotten about it. She returned his smile weakly, too satiated and exhausted to do any more than that, thinking how sweet he was to get dressed and go out in the snow for her. When he'd gone, she lay in his bed, looking around his room, feeling oddly warm and safe, yet needy. She needed him back with her, back in her arms.

A while later, she didn't know how long, she heard the door open. She kept her eyes shut, but could tell he'd come back into the room from the momentary chill that came in with him.

"Were they out there?" she asked.

"As luck would have it, they were coming up the street right when I reached your car. They got it started and said if I let it run for fifteen minutes or so it would charge the battery and should still start in the morning, so that's what I did. If it doesn't start, I can take you home."

But Summer was already way past car concerns. "Are you taking your clothes back off?" she whispered.

"Will you keep me warm?" he asked in the same teasing tone.

"Mmm," she breathed.

She waited as he undressed and climbed back beneath the blankets. She shivered at the touch of his cold skin, but they wrapped their arms around each other until he was warm, and then they fell asleep, embracing.

SUMMER DIDN'T KNOW how long she'd slept, only that when she opened her eyes, she still felt it, that strange, overpowering sensation of warmth and safety in Brett's arms.

She looked at him sleeping—dark lashes, mouth half-open, gentle breathing, his arm looped comfortably around her waist. She swallowed back a jolt of emotion too great to name. What had she done here?

Well, she knew what she'd done. She'd had the most spectacular sex of her life with a wonderful, marvelous man.

And she'd also done the one thing she'd promised herself she'd *never* do—she'd let herself begin to care. More than that, she'd completely lost control. Of everything.

The measure of safety she experienced in his arms left her weakened. She felt almost as if she needed him, and she *couldn't* need him. Besides being impossible—considering that she'd only known him for a number of hours—it simply wasn't feasible within the boundaries she'd set for herself.

Come on, Summer, keep a grip on your emotions here. Nothing makes you feel weak, and this is no time to let some guy suddenly do that. Get your control back...you have to. Remember, the last time you loved somebody, they needed you so much it ruined your dreams.

Damn it, she'd come too far since then to let anyone hold her back again, to let anyone take away the precious control she'd assumed over her life. It didn't matter what Brett had made her feel. She didn't need that. She didn't.

Control, she told herself. *Get it back.*

She took a deep breath, then felt a hint of it returning, a hint of the discipline and restraint so necessary to her life edging its way back into her heart. With it came a sense of relief.

Still, a tear trickled down her cheek as she eased away from him in the bed, and her stomach wrenched when their bodies separated completely. *Get the hell out of here,* her heart was screaming. *Get out while you still can.* Even as she relocated her ever-precious control, it didn't succeed in blotting out everything that had just happened.

Reaching around the bed, she gathered as many of her clothes as she could find. She ended up with everything except her panty hose, but that didn't matter. She crept to the living room, where her blouse and jacket lay in a heap on the floor with her coat, and got dressed in the dark.

Finally pulling her coat on, she had the gnawing urge to go back and look at him one last time before she left, but she ignored it. She needed control here. And time, too. With time, what she'd felt tonight would fade into obscurity, where it belonged.

Finding her keys next to her purse on the kitchen table, Summer grabbed it all up and sneaked out the door, still listening to the cries inside her that said, *Get out of here now, before you lose your heart.*

She descended the stairs and walked to her car through the fresh-fallen snow, and she kept her hands stuffed in her pockets, trying not to remember the way he'd kept them warm.

2

A MONTH HAD PASSED since that night.

A month that seemed like an eternity, and like no more than a day.

A month in which the cold snows of February had given way to the sharp winds of March, but the ground was still frozen outside, and that's how Summer felt, too. She could still remember his arms around her, keeping her warm, and yet everything had changed since that night. *Everything.*

Now Summer sat waiting for him in the same bar. Music came from speakers somewhere above, and three guys played pool at the table in the corner. She wanted to bite her nails. She wanted to wring her hands. She couldn't believe she was doing this, meeting with him like this. Her only hope for retaining her sanity was if he didn't show.

No, don't think that way, she told herself. *Remember, you're in control here. Just hang on to it through this meeting and then it'll all be over, forever.* Or at least a big part of it would be.

"What can I get you, sugar?" It was the same middle-aged waitress who'd served her the last time. Only then did Summer realize she sat in the very same booth. The urge to wring her hands grew stronger.

"A chardonnay, please," she said automatically. "No, wait," she added. "Just an iced tea."

She hadn't wanted to call Brett. In fact, she'd refused to. Tina had actually been the one to place the call, and not until she'd convinced Summer that it was the only decent thing to do. Deep down inside, she knew Tina was right, but at the moment, she regretted it. At the moment, she regretted a lot of things. Among those regrets was being here at all. What if things didn't go as planned?

BRETT DECIDED TO WALK the few blocks to Dunbar's. Taking to the sidewalk, he glanced at the white sky above. Looked like snow. He turned up the collar on his jacket to keep the wind off his neck, then stuffed both hands in his pockets.

He still had no idea why Summer wanted to see him. In fact, he'd considered not even going, but curiosity alone had been enough to change his mind. Tina had sounded so damned cryptic on the phone yesterday; "Summer needs to see you.... I can't say what it's about, only that it's important.... Yes, I know she snuck out in the middle of the night, but you have to push that aside."

He released a heavy sigh at the memory of waking up the next morning alone, of having opened his eyes expecting to see her, and finding nothing but an empty pillow beside him, of elation turning so quickly to emptiness. What could she possibly have to say to him now, a month later, that was so damned important?

Was this going to be some big I'm-so-sorry-but-I've-changed-my-mind-now kind of thing? Turning it over in his brain, he decided no way. Not Summer Avery's style. Besides, he thought wryly, Summer was too busy with her job to even see him again. Wasn't that the ridiculous story she'd tried to shove off on him? *Well, babe, if you* are *coming back begging for forgiveness, you can just forget it.* It just so happened that he had a life and an important job, too—one that had just gotten a lot *more* important—and this would be the worst possible time for him to get involved with anyone.

A few months from now, he'd be in Paris working with master architect Andre Bruseaux, designing the largest glass office building in the world. It was the opportunity of a lifetime, the kind of offer that came along once and changed your career forever. Brett was only thirty-two, so his career was still new, fresh, and this was the beginning of something huge. He still couldn't quite believe Bruseaux had chosen *him*, but he had. The call had come in from Bruseaux himself just last week. After interviewing architects all over the world, he wanted Brett for the project. *So there, Summer Avery,* he thought, feeling smug. *You're not the only one with an important job.*

Some of his anger had faded by the time he reached the bar. Or maybe it didn't really fade, maybe it was just overridden for a moment with the memories of their night together. Not just the sex part, which had been beyond great, but also the laughing-talking parts, their game of pool, the nachos and wings they'd shared. He'd have been willing to bet Summer Avery didn't get her fingers all greasy for just any guy. Not that any of it mattered now. She'd made her feelings for him clear enough before morning had come.

He took a deep breath, opened the door of the bar and stepped inside. Low music met his ears as he shook off the cold and looked around the room.

There she was, sitting at the same table where he'd met her. It was like a flashback to that night, except she wore a bright red suit this time instead of the olive one—

a power suit, he decided. And the sparkle that had lit her gaze completely by night's end had definitely disappeared now, leaving behind the cool, decisive eyes he remembered from the beginning.

Their gazes met across the room, catching him in a weird combination of desire and animosity. He walked over and sat down on the other side of the booth without taking off his jacket and also without speaking. He casually propped one elbow on the table and rested his chin atop his fist, all without taking his eyes off her. Damn, she was still beautiful. But it didn't matter. A lock of hair fell across his eyes, and he didn't bother pushing it away.

"Thank you for coming," she said. To his surprise, her voice actually trembled. Was this the same sedate woman he'd met that night? Even when he'd broken down her defenses and they'd made love, he didn't recall her voice ever trembling.

"Sure," he said shortly. "What can I do for you?"

He watched her take a deep breath, as if something huge lay at hand. What the hell did she want already? He was beginning to get a little worried, beginning to wish he'd followed his instincts and not come.

"It's, um, like this," she said. "I'm pregnant."

If Brett's fist hadn't been propping up his chin, his mouth would have dropped open. *She was pregnant?* This was *not* what he'd expected, or even imagined in his wildest dreams. He wanted to say something, anything, but remained too stunned. How could this be?

"Please understand that I'm not telling you this because I want money or anything else from you. I'm not seeking a commitment of any kind." Suddenly, she spoke very fast. "The only reason I'm here is because

Tina insisted that letting you know was the decent thing to do and, despite myself, I decided she was right."

There, she thought. She'd said it. The whole thing. Summer's heart pounded a mile a minute, but at least now the only part left was the waiting. *Please, God, let him just accept it and leave. Please let it end right here.*

"So you're saying," he began slowly, "that you're pregnant, and I'm the father." His eyes looked glassy with astonishment.

"That's correct," she told him. *No strings,* she wanted to add. *You're free to go.* But that seemed too pushy. Let him see it for himself. Let him understand that this was nothing more than a courtesy announcement, that nothing was expected of him.

"I used a condom," he said.

The words overwhelmed her when she'd least expected it, made her remember, practically *feel* him inside her, condom or not. *Damn it, pull yourself together, Summer.* "I know," she said, managing to sound surprisingly calm. "I told the doctor that. She said we must just be one of those dreaded ten percent for which they fail."

Slowly, he nodded, but Summer couldn't quite tell if what she'd said was really sinking in. God knew it had taken a while for *her* to come to grips with it, to believe it. God also knew it hadn't been what she'd planned at all, but she'd quickly resigned herself to raising the baby alone, and she only hoped Brett wouldn't decide to come to her rescue and do something honorable. The last thing she needed right now was a knight in shining armor.

"Wow," he finally said, his warm blue eyes finding hers again. "This is...pretty shocking news."

"I know," Summer replied, trying to ignore those eyes and the way they chipped away at her sense of control already. Breaking their gaze, she decided to reiterate. "And as I said, I'm only telling you because it seemed like I should, because it seemed like you should know. But you're..." Saying this part was kind of hard, because it sounded so cold.

He leaned forward a little. "What? I'm what?"

Oh hell, she thought, *quit beating around the bush.* "You're off the hook," she told him bluntly. "I want to raise the baby alone. I don't need any financial help. I don't need..." Oh, why did she keep letting her voice trail off?

He tilted his head, his eyes curious. "A father in the picture?"

She released a heavy sigh of admission. "Right," she said. "I don't."

"I see."

She wished she could read his expression, but his eyes suddenly seemed shrouded again. Well, she'd blurted out everything else, she may as well blurt this out, too. Anything to end the tension. "Is that all right with you?"

Brett took a deep breath, trying to absorb everything she'd said. Was that all right with him? He couldn't quite think straight. All he knew at the moment was that she'd left him in bed and now she wanted to leave him again, quick as that. This woman was definitely rough on a guy's ego.

He remembered thinking he should stay away from her. He wished to hell he'd taken his own advice, but none of that mattered now. All that mattered was that she sat across from him looking beautiful but rigid and waiting for an answer, an answer she'd already supplied him with herself. She wanted nothing to do with him. How could he argue with that? "Sure," he finally said, attempting to sound unaffected. "If that's what you want."

"It is."

"All right then."

The decision made, everything turned even more awkward than it already was, and before Brett knew it, Summer was out of her seat, reaching for the coat she'd tossed across the back of the booth. "Well, thank you," she said, without meeting his eyes. "I appreciate...your cooperation."

The consummate businesswoman, he thought. One more professional agreement made. He didn't reply, having no idea what to say, think, feel. He went numb watching her button her coat, reach for her purse, then go walking across the floor in her sensible heels. She left without looking back.

And Brett felt...empty. Even emptier than the morning after their night together, and he'd felt pretty damn empty then.

This was...too much. Too unbelievable. Too unreal.

She was having his baby. *His* baby.

And he'd just told her it was all right with him for her to raise that baby, *his* baby, alone.

What the hell had he been thinking?

AFTER SHEDDING HER SUIT and panty hose and slipping into an old pair of sweatpants and an oversize sweatshirt, Summer went to the kitchen, where she intended to make herself a nice salad—the first step in a plan for eating healthier while she was pregnant.

She briskly dug out all the ingredients from the fridge, then found a medium-size bowl. She worked quickly, slicing a head of lettuce into four wedges, doing the same to a tomato, using a peeler to shred a carrot, grating two different kinds of cheese and speedily slicing a hard-boiled egg into tiny pieces over top of her culinary creation.

She tried to concentrate on the salad without thinking about anything else, and had apparently tricked herself into believing that the faster she moved, the more she could block out her thoughts, but it wasn't working. She'd gotten out of that bar in the nick of time, just before Brett had taken her control again. Her breath caught simply from having his name flit through her mind.

She couldn't quit recalling the tiny pinch in her heart when he'd said sure, he'd let her raise the baby alone. That was exactly what she'd wanted, what she'd even prayed for, so why did it hurt?

She sighed as she reached for the box of croutons in an overhead cabinet. Maybe she hurt for her baby, but that was why she hadn't wanted him or anyone else involved in the first place. She planned to be all the baby needed, ever.

And no, this certainly wasn't the way she'd mapped things out, but considering that she couldn't exactly turn back the clock, she'd done the only thing she *could* do, and decided that it would be fine.

She had it all worked out in her mind. She made plenty of money, so she could afford a good nanny, whom she planned to start looking for over the next few months. Summer got three weeks of vacation each year, so she and her child would take fabulous trips together, to the beach, and in a few years, skiing. Eventually, maybe Europe. Her parents had both died during her college years and she'd been an only child, so she wouldn't have any family support, but as self-sufficient as she'd become, it was probably better that way. She would raise her child on her own without anyone's interference. And it would be wonderful.

Sitting down at her dining room table, salad and fork in hand, Summer thought of her mother. Would she be surprised to find out her only daughter was having a baby? No, in fact, she probably wouldn't be nearly as surprised as *Summer* still was. On her deathbed, Donna Avery had asked her about the future, and Summer had reeled off a pack of comforting lies about settling down and raising a family. After all, it hadn't been the time to point out that her dreams had been crushed by her commitments to her parents. Or to explain that she planned to devote herself completely to building a career in the fashion industry one way or another, which had meant she would likely never marry, never have children.

Oh, she didn't *blame* her parents for the dreams she'd had to give up—she'd loved them. Although they'd shared a long, happy marriage, it had taken almost twenty years for them to conceive a child, and the doctors had called it a miracle, so they'd looked on Summer as a precious gift and given her as wonderful a childhood as any parents could. But at the end of both their lives, things had grown very difficult for Summer.

She found herself wishing now, as she often did, that her mother could see what she'd managed to make of herself, even if it wasn't what she'd promised on that sad day. She was the youngest senior buyer in Stafford's history, and it was a demanding job, a job that often forced her to work late and on the weekends, a job that sometimes left her pulling her hair out. But more important than any of that was the fact that she loved it. She'd not had the chance to become the fashion designer she'd dreamed of being as a girl, but at least she got to choose and buy the clothes people wore. It came as close to satisfying her old, unreached dreams as anything could.

A small smile claimed her at the thought of picking out baby clothes, and later toddler clothes and clothes on up the age ladder. She'd been so consumed with making these huge decisions about the baby that she'd had little time to think of the fun parts yet. And it *would* be fun.

And now she didn't have to worry anymore about Brett Ford messing things up—her life, her child's life. She didn't have to worry about caring for him, even as hard as it had been to just walk out and leave him behind. Twice. Having accomplished that, she knew nothing would stand in her way. She would run her life as she wished, even now that a baby had been added into the equation.

She'd just gotten up from the table, carrying her empty salad bowl, when the doorbell rang. Hmm, was it Girl Scout cookie time? No, that had been last month. She padded to the door, flipped the lock and opened it...then wished she'd checked the peephole. Her mouth dropped open at the sight of Brett Ford. Oh no, what was *he* doing here?

"How do you know where I live?" she demanded.

"I looked you up in the phone book. Avery, S."

She swallowed. "What do you want?"

His expression turned surprisingly sheepish. "I should do this right," he mumbled.

"What?" she asked.

To Summer's immense surprise, he dropped to one knee and took her free hand in his. "Summer, will you marry me?"

She simply stared at him, stunned. "Huh?"

"Marry me," he repeated. "I want you to marry me."

This couldn't be happening. Really. It couldn't. "You're kidding, right?"

"Nope."

"You must be."

"I'm really not."

Summer was aghast. "What can you possibly be thinking?"

"That I want to be a father to my child," he said. "That I want him to have every advantage, like, for instance, a family. And that I think we can do this, that we can really make this work, and be happy."

A tiny, miniscule part of Summer was more touched than she'd ever been in her life at the sentiments he'd just expressed, but the other ninety-nine percent of her truly thought he must be out of his mind! Was he absolutely crazy? She'd feared he might want to take part in her child's life, but never in her worst nightmares had she anticipated that he might want to *marry* her.

"Please stand up," she told him, suddenly anxious to get him out of the proposal stance.

Hesitantly, he did so. She shook her hand free of his and tried to figure out the best way to approach this, which was difficult to do while suffering such outlandish shock.

But as her shock gave way to emotion, she couldn't help feeling a little soft inside. She couldn't marry him, of course, yet it was hard to look into those blue eyes for very long without getting a little mushy. My God, he'd come over to her house to propose marriage. The least she could do was be nice to him.

"I can't marry you, Brett," she said. "And I think it's sweet of you to ask, but like I told you back at the bar, I don't *want* to get married."

"I'm glad you think it's sweet," he told her, "but that's

not why I'm doing it. I'm doing it because I want to be a real father. I don't want to be a weekend dad. I don't want my kid to come from a broken home before even giving it a chance. Think about that. I had a good, solid family growing up, and I'm still very close to them. The fact is, I don't know who I'd be without them. I want to give my child that same opportunity. I know it sounds crazy, Summer, believe me, I do. But you and I, that night, we were good together and you can't deny it. I know one night doesn't seem like much to hang a marriage on, but the way I see it, it's all we've got to work with. So I'll ask you again. Marry me, Summer."

Summer stood before him, completely flabbergasted. She'd thought her simple, polite refusal would be enough to make him see reason, but apparently it would take more. He'd actually given this some thought and was deadly serious about it, which made dealing with it seem like a considerably larger challenge. This really, really could *not* be happening.

"But...my God," she uttered, "we don't even know each other."

"It felt like we knew each other that night," he replied quickly, smoothly. His voice was like warm honey pouring over her, and Summer felt herself flush at the weakening memory of them together. *Control*, she told herself. *Keep in control.*

With that thought in mind, Summer managed to rein in her emotions and remember how crazy all this was. The irony of it was unbelievable. Pregnant women everywhere were trying to get guys to marry them, and as probably the only single, pregnant woman in the world who wanted nothing to do with marriage, she couldn't get rid of the guy.

"Don't you get it?" she asked, incredulous and feeling

a little crazed. "This is a man's dream come true! A woman who's willing to let you off the hook—no ties, no promises, no money! You got me pregnant, but I'm not going to hold you accountable for it! Wake up! Most guys would kill for this!"

"I'm not most guys," he said matter-of-factly, obviously unaffected by her tirade.

"That's becoming quite clear to me," she replied.

"So what do I have to do to get you to change your mind?" he asked, as if it were a very simple question.

She released a sigh of exasperation. "It's just not possible."

"Why?"

She enunciated with care. "It's like I told you. I don't—"

"You don't want to get married, I know. But why?" His expression turned heart-wrenchingly earnest. "Whatever you're afraid of, Summer, I'll find a way to change it. I promise. Give me a chance."

Still, earnest or not, Summer had had it! What did she have to do to get this guy to give up and go away? She'd tried to reason with him, then she'd practically thrown a tantrum. What would it take?

"Listen to me and listen very carefully," she said, her anger rising. He was doing his best to break through her control, and she simply refused to let it happen! "I cannot marry you! I will not marry you! Not in March! Not in April! Not in May or in June! Not in a church! Not in Las Vegas! Not in a—a hot air balloon! No matter what you say, no matter what you do, I *cannot*, and *will not*, marry you!"

And at this, he laughed!

"What's so funny?" she demanded, stomping her foot on the floor.

"You sound like Dr. Seuss on a bad day," he said, still looking vastly amused.

She sighed, mentally exhausted, and sad, too. Eventually, he quit laughing, even smiling, seeming to tune in to her emotions. Their eyes met, and she wanted to look away because of the way his gaze affected her, but she didn't. If she could live through the next couple of minutes, she told herself, she'd never have to look on those eyes again. "Listen," she said quietly. "I really, truly cannot marry you, Brett. For reasons that are, frankly, not your business. We had sex, and it was nice, and we did what we were supposed to do to prevent pregnancy. But it didn't work, and now I'm going to have a baby. Let me repeat that. *I'm* going to have a baby. My entire life is changing and I'm dealing with it the best way I know how. That doesn't include *you*, or *marriage*. I'm sorry, I really am, but that's the way it is. Do you understand?"

He took a long, deep breath before drowning her in his dark blue gaze once more. "Yeah," he said, "I understand. But that doesn't mean I'm giving up."

With that, he placed his hand on the back of her neck and drew her to him. His kiss was deep and thorough, and just as intoxicating as Summer remembered. Oh God, she could drown in the warm, deep sweetness of it, of him, as he sensually devoured her with his mouth, his tongue exploring hers.

When he finished, she was breathless, and awakened to the fact that this was all much worse than she'd originally understood. This went beyond his having the ability to take away her control. Every time she was around him, it happened—everything she thought she knew about herself evaporated like spring dew beneath the morning sun.

He looked into her eyes, no doubt seeing the horrible desire that lurked there. And without another word, he turned and walked away, leaving her standing in the doorway, desperately clutching a dirty salad bowl and battling the overwhelming confusion that had just invaded her heart.

3

BRETT SAT BEHIND HIS DESK at work, twirling a pencil between his fingers. He wasn't sure what had gotten into him, but he'd meant every word he'd said to Summer the other night.

After she'd dropped the bomb, it had taken him a little while to fully absorb it, but then he'd realized that he was...*happy!* He was going to be a father! A *daddy!* And he wanted to marry her, have a child with her, make a family with her.

His own family meant everything to him, and he refused to let any child of his grow up without that same connection. His dad had been the cornerstone of his childhood, and because Brett had been the only boy in a family full of girls, the two of them had shared a special closeness. He couldn't imagine his life without his dad—through thick and thin, his father had always been there, and Brett had never taken that for granted. So he also couldn't fathom the idea of his child being fatherless when he was so ready and willing to be a dad.

As for loving Summer, he didn't know that he didn't. He definitely thought he could. They just didn't know each other well enough to say for sure.

And he intended to change that, right now.

Rummaging around his desk, he located the slip of paper with her work number on it; he'd asked his secretary, Anna, to call Stafford's and track it down for him this morning. Picking up the phone, he dialed.

"Summer Avery," she answered on the first ring. God, even over the phone, she sounded beautiful.

"Brett Ford," he replied.

A stunned moment of silence followed, then, "Oh."

He hated how taken aback she sounded, but in a way, he liked it, too. "Surely you didn't think I'd disappeared for good," he said.

"Well, when I didn't hear from you for a few days, I hoped that maybe you had."

Okay, that one jolted him, but he bounced back quickly. "I'm not going to let that hurt my feelings, Summer. Instead, I'm going to ignore it and ask you to lunch today."

She released a small, disgruntled breath on the other end of the line. "Lunch? Today? No, that's impossible."

"Because?"

"I'm very busy."

"You've got to eat, Summer."

"Don't tell me what I've *got* to do," she snapped.

"Think of the baby," he said softly.

Another tiny, stunned silence gave Brett a moment to feel the strange yet bonding connection they now shared. A baby. A living child, inside her, made by them both.

"Oh. Right," she finally said. "Well, I generally eat at my desk. Someone goes out for sandwiches."

Brett took a deep breath. Damn it, he just wanted her to give him a chance. Was that asking so much? "How about if I'm the someone who brings the sandwiches today?" he suggested.

"Brett, no."

"Why not? Summer, I just—"

"I can't have lunch with you, Brett. Now I have to go. Goodbye." The line went dead, leaving the dial tone to blare in his ear.

Brett sighed as he hung up the phone. One thing seemed clear—dealing with Summer Avery was going to get very frustrating, very quickly.

So she wouldn't have lunch with him, huh? *Well, this is okay,* he told himself. *This was just your first shot. You've got lots more left in you.* And he tried to ignore the tiny knife that twisted in his heart at her refusal to even see him.

In the meantime, he had other business to attend to, *important* business. This next move would be hard, but it was entirely necessary. The moment he'd realized he was going to be a father, there'd been no question about it. He left his desk and walked down the hall to Mr. Foster's office, knocking lightly on the open door.

"Brett, come in," Mr. Foster said cheerfully as Brett stepped inside. The middle-aged man was all smiles. That's how it had been ever since the Andre Bruseaux deal had come through. Mr. Foster and Mr. Hardin had always liked Brett, but now they were his biggest fans. "Sit down. What can I do for you?"

Brett took a deep breath, knowing his boss's happiness was about to fade, but he had to do this—there was no other way. "Mr. Foster, I don't know how to tell you this, but...I'm going to have to back out of the Paris project"

Mr. Foster simply stared at him, wide-eyed, and Brett thought the man's graying hair might have just gone a shade lighter.

Trying to ignore the look of horror on Mr. Foster's face, he went on. "I've had some unexpected news in my life. I'm going to become a father, and I might be getting married. So, needless to say, I need to be here."

Mr. Foster drew in his breath, raised his eyebrows, then released a long, drawn-out sigh, a reaction that seemed anticlimactic after facial expressions Brett had feared would lead to some kind of explosion. "I suppose that congratulations are in order then," Mr. Foster finally said, but he didn't exactly sound celebratory.

"Thank you, sir," Brett replied humbly, although he felt more apologetic than appreciative. "I'm sure you understand how hard it is for me to turn down the project, but as you can see, I have to."

"I'm certain you realize, son," Mr. Foster began, "that this isn't the kind of opportunity that comes along every day. You were handpicked, Brett, by Andre Bruseaux. *Handpicked.* Do you know what an honor that is?"

Brett attempted a small smile, but failed. Yes, he knew. He'd been reading about Andre Bruseaux's design innovations in industry magazines for the past ten years, and the man was the most sought after architect in the business. Brett knew all too well what he was turning down. "I understand the immense proportions of this decision, sir."

"Are you sure?" Foster asked him. "I mean, are you really sure? It's the difference between working in obscurity in this office for the next thirty years or having a global career that's every architect's dream. You're giving up the chance of a lifetime, Brett."

Brett swallowed. He knew all that, every damn bit of it, and he didn't especially need to have it pointed out to him just now. He took yet another deep breath and said, "Don't think I haven't given it a lot of thought, but this is my kid, Mr. Foster. I have to put him first. I need to be here when my child is born—nothing is more important." Whether Summer consented to be his wife or not, she was still having his baby, and he was determined to be here for his child, each and every step of the way.

Mr. Foster released another heavy sigh. "There's nothing I can say to change your mind then?"

"I'm afraid not."

Mr. Foster gave a short nod. "I do admire your dedication to your child, Brett," he said, sounding considerably more sincere now, but then he added the clinker. "So do you want to tell Andre or should I?"

"I'll do it," Brett replied. He didn't look forward to making the phone call, but it was the only decent thing to do...even if it would feel like hammering the nails into his own coffin.

Five minutes later, Brett sat behind his desk, dialing Paris. He wanted to deal with this all at once, while he was on a roll. His stomach wrenched with the enormity of what he was doing, but as he'd told Mr. Foster, he had to. Nothing else would feel right.

"Andre Bruseaux," said a sophisticated, French-accented voice on the other end of the line a few minutes later.

Brett tugged at his tie, which suddenly felt as though it was cutting off the oxygen to his brain. Then he steeled his resolve and explained to Mr. Bruseaux that he'd be unable to assist him in the design of the glass megatower as they'd planned. Unforeseen events had occurred in his personal life, he told the French architect, events that would prevent him from being away from the States. He decided to leave it at that since he didn't know Bruseaux well enough to start filling him in on the details. "So I'm terribly sorry," he concluded, "but you'll have to find someone else for the project."

A heavy silence hung between the men for a long moment until finally Mr. Bruseaux said, "You're the man I wanted for the job, Brett."

Damn, this was hard, and getting harder. Couldn't anyone just accept his decision without a fight? "I know and, as I said, I'm very sorry."

Bruseaux's sigh carried through the phone line, even an ocean away. "Well, if your circumstances should be altered, or if you should change your mind for any reason..."

Brett took a deep breath. He had to end this right here. "I won't."

BRETT SPENT THAT NIGHT lamenting the loss of his opportunity in Paris. He didn't eat dinner, he didn't watch TV, he simply lay on his couch thinking it through, over and over. No matter how he looked at it, though, the same answer prevailed. He had to be here, for his child, and for Summer, whether she wanted him or not. It was the only course of action that made sense to him.

The next morning after he arrived at work, he called her office again. After all, he'd just given up the "opportunity of a lifetime" for her. She was at least going to give him the time of day in return.

She picked up on the second ring. "Summer Avery."

Brett chose a different approach this time, taking the business tone out of the conversation. "Hi, Summer," he said. "It's me, Brett."

She released a heavy sigh, along with more of the silence that seemed to be her trademark on the phone. "Hi," she finally said.

But he wasn't going to give up as easily today as he had yesterday—he was too determined to make some headway. He leaned back in his desk chair. "Three guesses as to why I'm calling," he said playfully.

"I don't have time for guessing games, Brett. I'm very busy."

Don't let it get you down, buddy. Hang tough. "I want to take you to lunch today."

The pronounced *harrumph!* from the phone shook him slightly. "Brett, I don't mean to be rude—or maybe I do—but as I told you yesterday, I can't have lunch with you. I'm too busy."

"Tomorrow then?" he suggested. "Maybe you could clear an hour in your schedule."

"Not tomorrow," she told him. "And not any day."

"So basically, you're refusing to see me altogether."

"Yes."

Couldn't say she wasn't blunt, could you? Well, now that they had *that* straight... "Is there some reason why?"

"You *know* why."

Not exactly. "Because of my proposal? Or because I want to take part in my child's life?"

"The first one," she said. "Although the second one doesn't thrill me, either."

Brett took a deep breath and held his anger in check. He knew he had rights, but the last thing he wanted to do was play the legal card or start making threats. He didn't want this to be ugly, and he didn't want to frighten her. Even though her answer, combined with her tone of voice, had given him the distinct impression that he already had. "What are you so afraid of, Summer?"

"Me? Afraid? Hah!" He almost wanted to laugh at her silly bravado, but held it in and let her continue uninterrupted. "I'm not afraid of anything. You don't even know me well enough to presume I'm afraid."

"Well, you are," he said. "That's completely clear to me."

"I don't have time for this, Brett. I'm busy. Goodbye." Then came the dial tone.

Busy running away, he thought. But from what? Was he such a scary guy? All he'd done was profess his desire to be a husband and a father. Geez, most women would love that. What was it with *this* woman?

Well, he wasn't done yet—it would take more than hanging up to get rid of him this time. Without pausing, he punched in Stafford's main number. "Tina Conway please," he said to the operator.

"Hello, this is Tina," his old pal answered cheerfully a moment later.

"Hey, Tina, it's Brett."

"Hi, Brett," she said, but her voice already sounded apologetic—enough to tell him she knew everything that was going on.

"Listen," he said, "is she really too busy to have lunch with me?"

"She's busy, but...no, she's not *that* busy."

"Can you keep her there until noon today?"

"I guess. Why?"

"Because as much as I hate to be a pushy guy, I've just decided that she's gonna have lunch with me whether she likes it or not."

AN HOUR LATER, Summer sat in her office poring over the proposed fall line for juniors, but she couldn't concentrate. Usually she had a sixth sense about what trends would stay hot and which ones would not, yet today each garment looked the same to her.

It was all Brett Ford's fault, first interrupting her on the phone, now interrupting her thoughts, as well. *Con-*

trol, she told herself. *Keep hanging on to it.* It would be easy to let herself see him again, and *far* too easy to fall under the spell of those alluring blue-as-marble eyes, but she couldn't do it. She just couldn't.

Suddenly, above the sounds of keyboards and phone conversations outside her office's open door, she heard her receptionist stammering, "Um...can I, uh, help you?" The last two words came out sounding oddly flirtatious.

Summer glanced through the open blinds on the full glass wall that fronted her office and saw—oh my God— *Brett!* He carried a wicker basket looped over one arm like he was Little Red Riding Hood setting off to see Grandmother. "I'm a friend of Summer Avery's," he said smoothly, his voice warm and dark as melted chocolate.

"Did she, uh, know you were...coming?"

Summer stared. Besides the receptionist, Brett now garnered the attention of every other woman in the vicinity, and they were all practically drooling.

"No," he said, deep sexy voice intact. "I wanted to surprise her."

And as to why they were all drooling... Well, Summer didn't need to ask. He looked good. Really, really good. He'd looked good enough, in a cute, casual, confident sort of way, on the night they'd met—the night they'd...made love. But here, now, in an expensive, well-cut suit and silk tie, his dark hair touching the crisp white collar of his shirt, he was...*wow*. The word *debonair* came to mind. And if there was one quality Summer loved in a man, it was him being debonair—an affinity she'd picked up watching old black-and-white movies on TV with her mother when she was a little girl.

"Um..." The receptionist pointed vaguely toward

Summer's office, apparently too caught up in him to manage another word.

"Thanks," he replied, and then he even winked. The nerve, Summer thought, of him coming in here disrupting business, and then winking—*winking*—at her receptionist!

She stood up, prepared to do battle, when he walked in the door, shut it behind him, then pulled the blinds closed to immerse them in dusky privacy.

Summer swallowed. Battle wasn't as easy as she'd thought. Something stirred in her at the sight of his dark profile in her suddenly shadowy office, and she reached behind her to flip on the overhead lights she hadn't needed a moment ago. When she turned back toward him, he was looking at her.

"I liked it better in the dark," he said, a wicked grin playing about his mouth.

"I like it better in the light," she replied pointedly. Time for battle. "And I don't know what you think gives you the right to come marching in here, but—"

Before Summer could say another word, he was kissing her. She didn't know how he'd gotten around the desk so quickly, or why her body betrayed her so severely every time he was near, but she was melting, collapsing, being taken captive by his mouth, and his arms. Her entire body pulsed with desire as he skillfully plundered with his warm tongue between her lips, and just when she wondered how much more she could survive, he released her and took a step back.

"I brought lunch," he said with a smile. He said it so simply, as if he hadn't just completely wiped out her defenses, as if he hadn't just taken all her good senses, all her control, and tied it all very neatly into a tight, useless little knot.

"I hate you," she told him, but she knew it sounded far too tender. She also knew there was far too much longing in her eyes.

"No, you don't," he whispered, lifting a hand to her cheek, then leaning near her ear, his warm breath paralyzing her. "And I forgive you for saying it. I know you've got a lot on your mind.

"Now," he continued, letting his hand drop and losing the whisper, "lunch."

He reached for the basket he'd lowered to the floor upon entering and lifted it to her desk. Flipping open one side, he produced a red rose. Could anything possibly be more romantic? "For you," he said, holding it out. She took it. What else could she do?

Next, he pulled out two delicate wineglasses. "But—" she began to protest.

In reply, he lowered them to her desk and extracted a bottle. "Sparkling grape juice," he announced. "For the conscientious mother-to-be."

She couldn't help it then—she smiled.

Reaching back into the basket, he drew out grapes and cheese and crackers, and for dessert, two pieces of strawberry cheesecake in little plastic containers, leaving Summer astounded.

"Where did you..."

"The gourmet place in the Mercantile Center," he replied.

"Wow," she murmured. She was starting to come back down to earth a little, starting to remember how he'd barged in here, and how intent he seemed on barging into her life with or without her permission. Still, she had to admit..."This is nice."

"Summer, I know I'm being pushy," he said, reading her thoughts, "but all I'm asking for is a chance. So will you give it to me? Will you let me eat lunch with you to-day, let us get to know each other a little more? Please."

He seemed to know just how to soften her. She'd al-ready been well on the way to giving in, but the sweet "please" tacked on the end pushed her over the edge.

"All right," she sighed.

To her surprise then, Brett even fished from the picnic basket a red-and-white checkered tablecloth, which he unfolded and laid out on the floor of her office. They both sat down on it and spread the food between them, nibbling cheese and drinking grape juice as they talked.

Brett told her a little about his job—he'd been with his company for almost ten years and was very happy there. He found his work fulfilling, something she could relate to, and she found herself talking about her own job in re-turn. She explained her quick rise through the Stafford buying department and her recent promotion to senior buyer, pleased and even surprised that he was so im-pressed with her ambition.

When he asked about her house—the mid-size Cape Cod he'd visited the other night—she told him that she'd grown up there.

"Seemed like a nice place for a kid," he commented.

And oddly, his words reminded her that life had not always been so demanding. She didn't think about the days of her childhood often, yet thinking about them now, she quickly became lost in the reverie. "I've always loved that house," she said. "It's not a mansion or any-thing, but it's warm and it has a lot of character—I al-most think of it as having its own personality. There are all kinds of little nooks and crannies hidden all over the place, a huge walk-in pantry, a window seat in the up-stairs hall and lots of deep closets that slope with the pitch of the roof. I always thought of it like a big playground," she added, but stopped suddenly, realizing she'd babbled and wishing she hadn't.

Brett didn't even seem to notice, though. "Lots of good hiding places, I bet," he replied, grinning.

She returned his smile with a nod and felt almost as if she'd shared a secret with him.

"How did you end up with the house?" he asked.

The question reminded her that reality always beckoned, that some times in her life had *not* been so good. "I was an only child," she explained. "My parents had me late in life and both of them died while I was in college, so the house became mine."

"I'm sorry, Summer," he said. "That must've been hard—losing them both so close together."

"It was," she admitted. "Neither of them had any family, so I was kind of left on my own without anyone to turn to. It was rough for a while. Strange," she added, "to work so hard in school, wanting to make them proud, and then having no one to share it with in the end."

Summer went quiet then, wanting to kick herself. She hadn't planned on telling him anything personal, and to make it worse, she'd just experienced that odd, pulling sensation in her stomach that meant she'd *felt* something in telling him...something emotional. She simply couldn't have that. Not now, not with Brett Ford.

"But life goes on and so do I," she concluded, forcing herself to sound cheerful. "Enough about that. Tell me more about your job."

Brett complied, turning the discussion to architecture, and a few minutes later he changed the topic of conversation again. "How are you feeling, Summer?"

It caught her off guard. "Huh?"

"I mean, physically. With the baby."

Oh. She hadn't expected that. In fact, she'd almost forgotten it was what they had in common, and the reason he was here in her office, wooing her. She sighed, annoyed to remember that this wasn't true romance since he had an ulterior motive and was instantly tempted to tell him that how she felt was none of his business. She wasn't accustomed to accounting to anyone for her health, and it was disconcerting to have this man she hardly knew asking her about it.

However, it *was* his business, and she really wasn't all that mad at him for asking. Under any other circumstances, she might even have found it sweet of him to be concerned. "I've started having morning sickness," she confessed. "Except I don't get it in the morning. Sometimes it hits me in the afternoon, and other times at night."

"Is it really bad? I've heard it can be horrible. I have older sisters who've had babies," he added with a crooked grin that still managed to seem debonair as he lounged on the floor of her office in what she now recognized as an Armani suit.

"No," she lied, "it's not too bad." In actuality, Summer had found morning sickness to be pure misery, but she refused to take a chance on stirring up Brett's sympathy—she was getting far too much attention from him already.

"Well, if you need anything, or if I can be of any help during the pregnancy," he said, "please let me know."

"That's...nice," she said uncertainly, unable to meet his eyes now that their talk had turned back to her pregnancy. "But I'll be fine, thanks."

"So you're due in November," he said.

She shifted her gaze unthinkingly to his. "How'd you know?"

He shrugged. "We met last month, in February, and I can count to nine."

"Oh," she replied, feeling silly.

"Well," he said a few minutes later, "I'd love to stay here and talk to you all day, Summer, but I've already taken an hour and a half, so I'd better get back to the office."

She nodded, unable to believe how fast the time had gone or how much she'd let herself enjoy it, in spite of her many misgivings throughout. "I need to get back to work, too," she said.

Together, they packed the remains of their meal back into the basket, and both of them rose to their feet. Summer felt a little awkward, and she thought Brett suddenly looked like he might feel that way, too. "Just one more thing before I go," he said.

"What?"

"Will you marry me, Summer?"

Well, that hadn't come out seeming awkward at all. In fact, the words flowed over her like warm, dark velvet, his smooth, deep voice perfect for the kind of proposal you might hear in a fairy tale. In the depths of her soul, Summer suffered a delightful twinge that hovered between pleasure and pain, but in her brain it was the pain that took over.

She released an agonized sigh, shaking off any remnants of the fairy-tale feeling, since this was reality. Why did he have to bring this up again, right when their relationship had started becoming somewhat tolerable? Why had she let him persuade her to eat lunch with him at all?

She nearly wanted to cry as she said, "No, Brett. I won't marry you."

Almost as if he hadn't heard her, Brett lifted a hand to

her cheek and placed a long, slow kiss on her lips. Unable to resist returning it, she felt lost to him, consumed by him, until finally he pulled away. He met her gaze with those incredible blue eyes, then leaned in again, warm breath whispering in her ear. "You like my kisses."

When he pulled back to peer at her once more, she said nothing, too stunned for words. She wanted to deny the accusation, but her body betrayed her as exquisite tingling sensations raced up and down her spine.

"When I kiss you," he said tenderly, "I feel everything you're not saying."

"Which you believe to be?" she dared ask.

"That this isn't all as cut-and-dried for you as you like to pretend. That you have feelings for me. Feelings you can't push away, Summer, or you would have by now."

Summer steeled her courage and remembered reality. "They're just kisses," she said. "They don't matter."

To her surprise, Brett flashed his crooked grin.

"Why are you smiling?"

"Because I don't believe it for a minute," he said, lowering his head for another quick kiss on her receptive lips before turning to go.

As he made his way to the elevators and disappeared inside, Summer watched from her office door, all the while trying to ease the achy tension that had grabbed hold of her entire body. Then she shut her door and went behind her desk, where she collapsed in her chair.

She had a very serious problem here.

This guy wanted to marry her.

And this guy's kisses were...*incredible.*

He wanted to invade her life—permanently—and she had to figure out how to stop him while wanting him like she'd never wanted any man before. Unfortunately, it was hard to be mean to him. She loved having him around and, as he'd so quickly surmised, she loved his kisses, too.

So why not just do what he wanted? she asked herself. Why not marry him? At least maybe date him officially?

No! she scolded herself. It would be too easy to love him, and when you loved people, you made sacrifices for them. You just *did*.

You did it because it was expected. And you did it because your heart made you, your heart told you it was right, what you had to do. Summer had already made enough sacrifices in her life, let enough people influence her choices, and—shameful as it felt—she'd resented it in the end.

Why was it so bad to just want to live alone with her child and make her own decisions and run her own existence by herself? And how long would Brett Ford keep tempting her to do otherwise?

A FEW WEEKS LATER, March had turned to April and Summer lay on the couch in her living room in oversize flannel pajamas, sulking.

The skirt she'd worn today had felt too snug, although she doubted she could be showing this early, and was probably just imagining it. Still, rather than make a big announcement to the department, she'd told Tina to please discreetly start telling people she was pregnant. Which meant having people question her situation. It reminded her of the way she herself had been questioning her body recently.

After all, a few weeks ago everything had been fine, her life had been completely normal, without worry or questions. But now her body was starting to change in ways she couldn't stop or anticipate, and people's perceptions of her were about to change, too. She had no control over any of it, and she just kept asking herself the same thing over and over: how had this happened? It was still hard to believe.

Brett had shown up at her office twice more with picnic lunches. Despite herself, she enjoyed his company, but each lunch had ended with the one thing she loved best and the one thing she dreaded most—a kiss and a proposal. The kiss she couldn't resist accepting. The proposal she continued to turn down.

What was it with this guy? Why wouldn't he take no for an answer? In one way, she could almost see his point—she didn't want her child to have only a weekend dad, either—but her original hope had been that the baby wouldn't have any dad at all, damn it. She'd wanted to raise the baby herself, her own way, and each time she examined the situation, she came to the same conclusion—she had to stick to her guns. She couldn't let someone enter her life as an equal partner, or *any* partner. She'd known that for years.

And on top of all her worries, she was sick. Really sick. She'd thrown up twice since getting home and now she lay on the couch just praying for the nausea to go away. How did other women survive this torture?

Just then, a knock came on the door. Oh no, who could it be? Summer lay there floundering in agony, eventually deciding not to answer. Whoever it was would just have to go away. If it happened to be a woman who had ever experienced morning sickness, she'd surely understand.

There was another knock, harder this time, and Summer squeezed her eyes shut, thinking, *Go away, go away*, as if willing them to leave might really work.

Yet the knock came once more. Why wouldn't people just leave her alone? What could be *that* important?

Gathering all her strength, Summer pulled herself up off the couch and wove an uncertain path to the door, muttering, "This better be some kind of emergency." She flung it open to find Brett standing on her porch with a pizza box in his hands and a smile on his face.

"I was hoping you hadn't eaten yet," he said.

What the hell was wrong with him, just standing there smiling at her like everything was fine? Didn't he know her entire world was upside down and that she felt like she might soon die? She wanted to slug him for putting her in this awful condition, but she was too dizzy. And the very thought of pizza made her want to wretch. She turned her head, trying to escape the aroma, saying, "Get that stuff away from me. I'm sick."

"Oh," he said, "I didn't know. I'm sorry."

"I've gotta lie down," she said, then turned and headed for the living room before she collapsed.

A moment later, Brett appeared at her side, kneeling next to the couch. As the profound wave of nausea passed for a moment, it occurred to her to wonder what he'd done with the pizza. And to also wonder what she looked like, besides a wreck.

He was stroking her hair and asking what he could do to help her, when she said, "Go away."

"Why?"

She was in too fragile a condition at the moment to remember to lie. "I don't want you to see me like this."

"See you like what?"

"Sick. I must look horrible." She wanted to cry.

He continued to caress her hair, then leaned in to lower a soft kiss to her forehead. "No, honey," he said in a tone so soothing that it managed to cut through all her anger and despair. "You're beautiful."

Oh God, he was calling her *honey* and saying she was beautiful. How incredibly sweet! "You're lying," she said anyway. "I look awful."

"No, honey, you don't. You're just sick. But you look fine, I promise. Now what can I do to take care of you?"

Summer released a long sigh, but not in irritation; it actually felt more like relief. Rather warm, rather good, like a dream of long-awaited rest. She couldn't help it. Despite herself, it was nice to be coddled by someone, especially now.

She had no family and few friends. She'd told Tina about the pregnancy, of course, but she'd refused any help from her, too, and kept the emotions to a minimum when talking about it.

Summer had been handling this alone, the same way she'd handled everything alone for a very long time now. Which was generally fine, because she was usually so strong, her losses during college having made her that way. But tonight her strength had started to wane a little. *So just this once,* she told herself. *Just tonight, I'll let someone be here for me.*

"I...was thinking about getting some crackers," she told him, "but I hadn't worked up the energy yet."

"Where are they?" he said, hopping to his feet.

"Pantry. First door on the right in the kitchen. Second shelf from the top."

"Anything else? Something to drink?"

"No, just the crackers."

Brett stripped off the spring jacket he wore and tossed it over the back of a chair—as if preparing for a long stay—and then disappeared into the kitchen, returning a moment later with a box of saltines. Summer reached for them when he knelt next to her again, but he said, "No, wait. I'll get them out for you." She watched patiently as he dug out a stack of crackers and opened the wrapper, offering her the first one on top.

"Thank you," she whispered numbly.

When a blanket fell over her body, she realized it was the throw she kept draped over the back of the couch. "What's that for?" she murmured.

"You looked cold."

She attempted a nod against her pillow. "Yeah, it was chilly in here when I got home. I kept meaning to turn up the heat, but the thermostat's all the way down the hall and it seemed like a long walk at the time."

"I'll go turn it up," he told her, heading quickly on his way.

"Brett?" she asked when he'd come back.

"Hmm?" He knelt in front of her again, watching her eat crackers.

"Where's your pizza?"

"Oh, that," he said, sounding sheepish. "I tossed it in the bushes outside."

She almost laughed, despite her aching stomach. "You tossed it in the bushes? Why?"

"It was making you sick," he reminded her.

"Why don't you go get it."

"No, it's all right. I don't want to make you feel any worse."

"I can handle it," she said. "It was just the combination of the smell along with standing up. I was dizzy and queasy, but now I'm just queasy, and the crackers are helping. So really, go get your pizza and eat some of it."

"Are you sure?"

"Completely."

Summer continued munching her crackers as Brett

went outside to get his dinner. When he returned, he sat beside her in an easy chair with a couple of pizza slices and a soda he'd gotten from the refrigerator. Summer couldn't believe how much better she felt, not just from the crackers, but to have someone else there, someone who seemed to care about her welfare. Even in the silence, she felt his presence, and she valued it more than she ever could have known or predicted. As she'd thought before, she was long overdue for a rest, and long overdue for letting everything go, even if just for a couple of hours.

"Brett," she said a little while later, "thank you...for being here."

He knelt next to her once more and began stroking her hair. God, it felt nice. *Too* nice. "I *want* to be here," he told her. "I want to take care of you."

Oh wow, he'd said it again—he wanted to take care of her. It still struck her as a strange and novel idea. She knew very well what it was like to take care of someone else, but the last time someone had been there to take care of *her*, she'd been a little girl. "That's...sweet," she told him. "I haven't had that in a very long time."

"Since your parents died, I guess," he whispered, his fingers still in her hair.

"Longer," she admitted. "For the last years of their lives, *I* had to take care of *them*."

"You did?"

She nodded slightly against the throw pillow beneath her head, thinking back to those days, her sickness dissipating just enough to clear the way for lucid memories. "When I was a senior in high school, my mom was diagnosed with lung cancer."

She watched as his eyes dropped. "God, I'm so sorry, Summer."

How many times over the years had she heard some combination of those words, of that consolation? Still, it didn't diminish the sentiment—she knew instantly that Brett really cared. "It's all right," she said. "I mean, it was very hard, but I've had a lot of time to adjust to it."

"So you took care of her," he said.

"Yes. I had...been accepted into Berman's, an exclusive fashion design school in New York, but I didn't get to go."

"Oh, Summer..." She could hear it in his voice, knew without doubt that he really understood her pain, and it compelled her to tell him more.

"I'd wanted to be a fashion designer since I was a little girl, but, of course, my parents came first. They had to. I went to college here instead, but none of the local schools had the classes I needed to seriously pursue design, so I took mostly business courses. Mom died at the end of my sophomore year, and by then my dad was sick, too."

She watched as Brett's eyes went wide, then she answered his unasked question.

"He wasn't ill with anything in particular, but like I told you, they had me late in life, and he was well into his seventies. He needed special care by then because his kidneys were failing and he just couldn't get around very well anymore. He died a month before I graduated."

"That sounds...really tough, Summer," Brett murmured gently.

Tough to lose her parents? Or was he talking about giving up her dreams? "Yeah. Pretty tough."

Leaning near her face, all sweet eyes and tender expression, he placed a warm hand on her cheek. "You did the right thing, you know," he whispered. "You did what you had to."

Oh God, talking about these memories—something she never did—was bringing it all back to her, bringing it all a little too close to home. Tears threatened as she looked up into his eyes. "I know," she replied softly.

"I understand now," he told her.

She sniffed and swallowed back the pain. "You understand what?"

"Why your job is so important to you, and maybe even why you don't want me in your life."

This startled her a little.

"You've gotten used to being alone and making your own way in the world. You've gotten used to answering only to yourself. You don't want to give that up. You don't want to take a chance on letting anyone stand in the way of your ambitions again."

Summer said nothing, stunned at his words. He'd read her like a book. Was she that transparent? Well, yes, she supposed that tonight in particular that description fit her perfectly. Just like the first day he'd come to her office, she hadn't meant to tell him her life story. She hadn't meant to say any of it, but his eyes were so caring and his touch so gentle. She'd been weakened already when he'd arrived, and his presence had served to weaken her even more.

She wasn't used to being so vulnerable, and yet it seemed since the moment she'd met Brett, she'd begun to lose her firm hold on...*everything*.

In fact, it was becoming frighteningly clear to her that Brett Ford was her Achilles heel, her *only* weakness, and what a big weakness he was. She didn't know whether he had the power to ruin her life or to make her the happiest woman alive—or both.

"I understand what you're feeling, Summer," he said. "Ambitions are important, and doing fulfilling work is important, but you have to remember that people are important, too. What it all comes down to in the end is the people who you love and who love you. You can't shut out every relationship in your life just because you're afraid of giving up your independence."

Oh, damn it, now he was saying her feelings were wrong? She wanted to cry again, but this time in frustration and anger. How dare he presume to analyze her? Why had she been stupid enough to open up to him in the first place?

"Can I tell you something?" he asked, interrupting her thoughts.

"All right," she agreed.

"I don't know where I'd be in life without my family's guidance and support, especially my dad's. And when I think of my childhood, I think of *him*. I think of sitting up late at the kitchen table putting model airplanes together. I think of tossing a baseball with him in the street in front of our house and of the pep talks he gave me on rides to my Little League games. I think of him helping me with my homework and reading me bedtime stories. I have all these wonderful memories of him and my family—Christmases, family vacations, lazy summer days in the backyard.

"Not a day goes by that I'm not thankful for the guy. I love it when he laughs at my jokes or when he acts impressed over the kitchen I installed. When I hear him bragging to one of his friends that his son is a damned talented architect, I feel proud to have made *him* proud."

His voice softened as he gazed into her eyes. "Can you imagine your life without either one of your parents, Summer? Even though you went through a rough time at the ends of their lives, even though it changed the course of your future, can you even imagine who you'd be without having had them? Can you imagine yourself without all the memories, all the little things—and the big things—that they gave you and did for you and taught you, all the things that turned you into who you are?

"Summer, I want those same good memories for my kid. For *our* kid." The sincerity in his eyes seemed to reach out and touch her. "I want him to have the fullest kind of life, with nothing left out, nothing missing. I want a chance to be the best dad in the world to him, and I want to ask you to try...just try...to open your heart to me. Just try to let me in a little. Give me a chance to love you. I know we can be happy."

If Summer had wanted to cry before, she really wanted to now. But was it in pain, or anger, or frustration? She didn't even know anymore. She only knew that she hovered on the brink of tears, suffused with more emotion than she'd let herself feel in a very long time, and she didn't understand why or what was happening to her or what she could do to stop it.

Brett's words were beautiful, and yet...what about all her vows of controlling her own life? She'd lived with those intentions for ten years and her goals were important to her. She'd never be a fashion designer, but she'd at least be the best at what she *did* do.

And what, in the beginning, she'd thought was about *her*—about her being cared for by him, about her daring to open up to him—had, in the end, turned into being about *him*. Him and his father, him and his need to *be* a father. Damn it, he didn't really care about her at all, did he? She couldn't make sense of it all, and her nausea was coming back and she just wanted to be like she'd always wanted to be—alone.

"Please go, Brett," she told him simply.

"What?"

He gaped at her, plainly puzzled by her reaction, but she didn't care. "I want you to go," she said. "To leave me alone."

"What did I do wrong, Summer?"

"Go, Brett. Leave. Now."

"But, Summer, please. Tell me. What did I do? I thought things were going good. I thought we were getting to know each other here. I thought—"

"Please don't make me ask you again," she said. She wished she could yell, yet she was too tired. She could sense his eyes boring into her, begging her to explain, but she dared not look at them, not now. "I want you to leave me alone, Brett, once and for all. No matter how you twist things or how sweet you can be, it doesn't change the way I want my life. I won't marry you, Brett. I just won't. Not ever."

4

BRETT SAT ON HIS COUCH looking over the new plans for
the ComEx building downtown. He scribbled some
notes on a pad of paper, details he needed to discuss
with his partners on the project, but his head wasn't really focused on the work. It'd been weeks since Summer
had thrown him out of her house, but he still couldn't
get her off his mind.

He lowered his pencil to the coffee table and leaned
his head back with a sigh. Visions of that night kept in-
vading his brain—how cute she'd looked in those big
pajamas, how gentle her eyes had been. And it wasn't
just visions; the *feelings* he'd experienced still haunted
him, too. When she'd opened up to him about her parents, he'd thought things were changing, thought they
were making some serious progress. He'd wanted to
crawl onto the couch with her, snuggle up, keep her
warm and cozy all night. He'd been sure they were making a real connection that would begin to draw them together *permanently*.

Then she'd thrown him out.

He'd spent the weeks since considering his options.
Continue to shower her with impromptu picnic
lunches? Continue to show up on her doorstep unan-
nounced and unwelcome? Nope. He'd been that route
and it hadn't worked. He planned to be there when his

baby was born, but in the meantime, he'd decided to leave her alone.

He didn't want things to be that way, but she obviously had plans of her own that didn't include *him*. He wished she would let him help her—God knew he understood about sacrificing, having just sacrificed a fabulous career opportunity for the sake of her and the baby—yet she clearly didn't want his help, with anything. He'd finally started getting the message, but he wished it were different, wished he knew how to *make* it different.

The hardest part about trying to let go of the idea of being a family, of being with her, was that something had happened over the few weeks they had spent together. Something big.

He'd started thinking about her constantly, wishing he could be with her every second, and each time she came to mind, he felt happy inside, even though she practically hated him. He still felt that way right now, damn it. He fantasized about making love to her again, but even just being near her was enough to warm his heart and make him think the world was perfect. The idea of making her happy became more than just a desire, but an actual need.

And he knew what all that meant—it was obvious. The same thing had happened with his first girlfriend, Robin, back in high school, and then again with Joni in college.

It meant—damn it—that he'd fallen in love.

SUMMER DROVE AROUND the block twice, spying on Brett's apartment. It was that dusky time of night, the time, she figured, that if people were home they would start turning on the lights inside. She didn't see any lights.

After a third trip past the place, she concluded that he must not be there, which made this a safe time to return the jacket he'd left at her house that night last month.

She actually trembled as she climbed the steps to his apartment. Memories of walking up these same stairs a few months earlier, and being careful not to slip on the snow that covered them, filled her mind. That's how all this had started. And she could see it *all*—the way he had made love to her, the incredible warmth she'd felt in his arms afterward. It was May now—the weather had warmed and birds chirped in the distance—but still Summer shivered.

Despite her longings for him, she remained glad that she'd asked him to leave, and glad he'd paid her no further surprise visits, too.

Not that she didn't miss him—she did. Yet she'd managed to make a clean break, and that was the important thing. If he popped back up later, ready to play daddy to her child, she'd deal with it, but at least his disappearance from her life right now meant that his silly marriage proposal had finally been forgotten, that he'd finally accepted her decision and moved on. It also meant, thankfully, that she didn't have to continue putting herself through the torture of saying no, no, no to his advances when her heart had other ideas.

She'd supposed she could just keep the jacket, since she'd probably be forced to see him eventually, like when the baby was born. But returning it seemed like a good idea, a way of saying to herself, *Yes, this is over.*

And just in case he *did* change his mind later and decide he *didn't* want to take part in the baby's life, returning the jacket ensured Summer that she'd have no reminders of him to deal with, that she'd simply be able to chalk him up as a mistake.

And maybe someday she'd actually be able to make herself believe that.

She'd intended to just leave the jacket on his stoop, in front of his door, but now that she stood there, it seemed like a bad idea. The stoop was dirty; it had rained yesterday and his welcome mat hadn't yet dried. She wanted him to see the return of the jacket as a considerate, albeit impersonal, act. To leave it on the wet stoop would just make her look *in*considerate.

Hmm, where else could she put it? She toyed with the idea of wrapping it around the wooden handrail on the landing, yet feared it would blow away if a good gust of wind came along. She even considered going downstairs and giving it to his landlady, but Summer really didn't want to go to that much trouble, or risk becoming any more enmeshed in his life.

Aha! Her eyes went wide as the solution struck her. She'd reach inside the screen door and hang it on the inner handle. That would work. It wouldn't blow away and it wouldn't be on the ground. Perfect.

She opened the door and slid the jacket over the small door handle until it hung suspended, then breathed a sigh of relief. Success! She could go now, with a clear heart.

Well, as clear a heart as possible under the circumstances. She was just glad to have returned the jacket—it seemed like an official ending to their "relationship."

When the inside door suddenly opened, Summer flinched. She raised her gaze to find Brett standing in the doorway.

Brett, mere inches away from her, his dark hair mussed.

Brett, wearing a T-shirt and pleasantly snug jeans with a rip in one knee.

Brett, looking his sweet, confident, easygoing self.

Well, except for one thing—his eyes. As warm and blue as ever, they didn't look happy, and he didn't greet her with his usual crooked grin, either. Instead, the two of them stood staring at each other, both frozen in place. Frozen in sadness, too, she thought.

"I...was just returning your jacket," she said. She looked at his chest, because she couldn't bear to meet his gaze. "You left it at my house...that night."

"You could have called me and I'd have picked it up. Or—" he glanced down at the way she'd hung it on his door handle "—you could've just knocked."

She'd been caught being childish. But she hadn't planned on being caught at all, so the only thing she could muster at the moment was a tiny shred of honesty. "I was trying to avoid seeing you."

She heard his sigh and glanced up in time to see the hurt pass through his eyes. "Look, I'm not an ogre," he said, "and you've made it more than clear where I stand, so you won't have to worry about me bothering you anymore. At least not on a romantic front."

Something in Summer's stomach shriveled. She'd drawn that conclusion already, of course, and felt quite relieved about it, but hearing him actually say the words wasn't easy.

"Does that mean," she asked, skipping ahead in thought, "you still plan to take part in the baby's life?"

"Yep," he said. "Afraid so."

Oh God, she hated his cynical tone. "I didn't mean—"

"Come on, Summer. We both know you don't want to share this baby with me, so don't tell me what you *didn't mean*. I plan to be there for the baby from day one, but I'll try to be as little a bother to you on a personal basis as I can. How's that?"

Summer didn't know what to say. She hadn't expected him to sound so cold. She hated how hurt he seemed, how angry, and her lips trembled as she spoke. "Brett, please don't be mad. I'm sorry I don't feel the way you want me to. I really am. But let's try—"

He cut her off with a burst of wry laughter. "That's hysterical," he said.

"What's hysterical?"

"The fact is, Summer, you *do* feel the way I want you to! You're crazy about me!"

She gasped at the accusation and took a step back. She almost couldn't believe what she'd just heard! What audacity!

"I can see it in your eyes right now," he continued, "so don't bother denying it. And if I'm angry, it's only because you keep lying about it. You won't even try to deal with it."

"But I—"

"Look, I've heard enough protests from you. What it all comes down to is this—you don't care enough about your child's happiness and welfare to try to get past your selfish need to be totally in control of every second of your life."

Now he'd gone too far! "How dare you accuse me of—"

"The thing you haven't realized yet is that control isn't always good," he spouted, cutting her off once more. "In fact, control can get downright boring, Summer. And being *out of* control can be wonderful sometimes if you only let it. Let me give you an example," he said, and he grabbed her wrist and pulled her in the door.

Before she could protest, he drew her into a quick, tight embrace and kissed her hard, stealing her breath. She felt faint beneath the onslaught of his desire, and her emotions ranged from resentment to passion. But no matter which emotion she looked to, she simply didn't possess the strength to push him away.

His tongue slid between her lips and explored her mouth with an urgency she'd never experienced with him, and before she could calculate what was happening, she found herself clutching at his neck, feeling the rough caress of his mouth all the way to her fingers and toes. She moaned beneath him, pressing her body against his, letting the hardness in his jeans push at the cleft between her legs, and she wanted more, oh so much more... She wanted all of him.

When he ended the kiss and pulled back, she forced her eyes open, but knew she couldn't begin to hide her just-been-kissed-into-oblivion longing. Their gazes met in a sultry connection that needed no words, but Brett chose to speak anyway. "See what I mean?" he whispered. "You just lost control completely, and you loved it just as much as I did."

Summer swallowed. What could she say? She came up with nothing, but their eyes stayed locked and she felt as if he could read every thought in her head, every ounce of confusion, every bit of desire. Weakness prevented her from masking any of her emotions.

"Give me a night," he said huskily, still holding her, his arousal still pressed at the juncture of her thighs.

"What?" she breathed.

"Give me a night to show you how good it can be between us."

"I'm not arguing that it's not good—"

"Give me a night to convince you that it's meant to be,

Summer. One night to show you how perfect our life together can be, if only you'll give in and let it happen."

"But, Brett—"

"And if, when you wake up tomorrow morning, you can honestly tell me you don't belong in my bed, in my life, I'll surrender completely. I'll be the most agreeable weekend dad you've ever seen and nothing more. I promise. Deal?"

Summer sighed. How could she think ahead to the morning? She could barely think at all. All she could do was feel him and want to feel more of him, want to absorb him into her skin.

She took a deep breath and met his heated gaze. "Deal," she whispered.

BRETT HADN'T MEANT TO yell at her, but he'd been so surprised to find her there, and hurt, too, that she would go to such lengths to avoid him. He hadn't planned to kiss her, or propose any such deal to her, either.

Now she was in his arms, accepting his advances, accepting *him.* A few minutes ago he'd been depressed as hell because he thought he'd never hold her again, and suddenly, here she was, gazing up at him with undisguised heat, each perfect curve of her body molded to his in invitation. It was too good to be true.

He brushed a kiss over her lips and felt the shudder snake through her. Good, he thought. He wanted her to shudder. He wanted to make her feel *everything.*

For the first time in his life, as he slid his hands over her back, down onto her bottom, he questioned how he should make love to a woman. Tender or rough? Or something in between? Damn it, since when didn't he just do what came naturally? After all, he'd never gotten any complaints.

But everything hinged on *this* lovemaking. His future happiness, and that of his child. In his heart, he believed Summer's happiness hung in the balance, too.

"I want you so much," he whispered. The words had tumbled from him almost involuntarily.

"I want you, too," she breathed.

The softly spoken sentiment wafted over him like a hot breeze, and his heart raced with the knowledge that, at least for tonight, she was letting go, letting herself want him as he'd always known she did deep down inside.

Sliding his hands around to the front of her body, he let his palms graze her breasts, then drop to the buttons on her suit. When finally he pushed the pale yellow jacket from her shoulders, a soft murmur escaped her. "I feel like I've been here before."

He understood that; three months ago they'd stood almost in this very spot while he'd begun to undress her. "But it's different this time," he whispered, nibbling her ear and undoing the first button on her blouse.

"Why?"

"Because this time I love you."

The words hung between them like a fragile lifeline, connecting them, but only tentatively. *Reach out and grab it*, Brett willed her. *Grab the lifeline and make the connection real.*

Like an answer to his unspoken wish, Summer hesitated briefly, then threw her arms around his neck and clung to him with a need he'd only imagined he might ever feel from her. He wrapped his arms around her just as tightly, crushing her against him as each nerve ending in his body exploded with love. *Thank you, God! Thank you!*

Things turned frenzied then as they fought with each

other's buttons and zippers, pulling at shirttails and other scraps of clothing until finally they stood in Brett's kitchen, blissfully naked. Summer trembled—from nervousness or desire, he didn't know, but he intended to make it the latter.

Stepping forward, he firmly clutched her bare bottom and lifted her onto the kitchen table, making her release a tiny squeal. Gazing into her eyes, letting the heat he saw there wash over him, he gently reached down and parted her thighs with his hands. Soft and pretty, she sighed as he took another step closer.

He cupped her face in both palms and studied her, this woman he loved, and he remembered the first time he'd seen her. He'd thought her cold and rigid then. He'd thought the same many times since. But right now she looked sweet and gentle and vulnerable, and after he lowered an unpredictably chaste kiss to her lips, he leaned near her ear and whispered, "I want to kiss you everywhere."

She pulled in her breath and let her eyes shut. Sweet acceptance of his promise. So he began.

He kissed her forehead, then each closed eyelid, her upturned nose. Sweeping a kiss tenderly across her lips, he watched the graceful arch of her neck and lowered his mouth there, as well, raining kisses across her throat, up toward her ear, then down to her porcelain shoulder.

She met each kiss with a lovely little gasp, but that changed when his mouth moved to the upper slope of her breast. Now her breath became softly labored, and he felt his arousal increase, knowing he delivered an exquisite torture.

He raked his tongue over one rose-colored nipple, hard as a pearl. She shuddered and he did it again. Soon he suckled her and her hands sunk into his hair, pulling him against her, silently begging him to continue. He wanted to take her, right then and there, but not yet, he told himself. Not yet.

Bending over her, he backed away from her breasts to kiss her silky smooth stomach, her tiny slit of a belly button. Then he kissed her lower, lower, his mouth edging its way to the patch of soft, tawny hair that protected her secrets. Drawing away, nearly trembling with his own hesitation, he dropped to his knees and began to kiss his way tenderly up one pale inner thigh.

He listened to Summer's breath, quivery and catching in her throat, and when he dared to lift his gaze, he found her watching him, biting her lower lip. He spread her legs even farther apart, opening her to him, then he swept his tongue slowly up her center.

She cried out and his blood raced. He wanted to make her feel incredible, wanted to take her to places she'd never been before. He imagined touching her soul.

He worshipped her with his mouth then; that was clearly what he was doing, how he was loving her. He used his tongue and lips, kissing and licking and sucking, and she writhed above him, whimpering and moaning and making him even crazier with wanting her. He'd done this once before with her, the first time they'd made love, but this was truly different. Then, she'd been a stranger, another lover. Now she was the woman he adored, the woman he wanted to be with...always.

She moved against him, her motions taking on a vibrant energy he felt to his core. Finally, her body tensed, her legs wrapping hard around his neck, and she cried out her passion in a beautiful rush of sound that encased him like hot, sensual music. Then she bent over him, pulling him up and hugging him tightly against her. He rested in her embrace, more fulfilled than he thought he'd ever been, even without a climax of his own.

"Nice?" he finally asked, lifting his head from her breast to risk breaking the silence.

"Mmm," she said, her eyes turned languid and glassy.

"Do you want me inside you now?"

"Oh yes," she replied, nodding softly, invitation in her gaze.

Brett rose up, dropping a short glance to the spot he'd just kissed so fervently, and as he entered her, as he felt her wrapping around him like a warm, tight glove, he released a deep, guttural moan.

Summer gasped at the hot, pleasant intrusion into her body. He felt so good inside her, so warm and so wonderful. She was still basking in the afterglow of his sweet mouth on her, and now *this*.

Somewhere in the back of her mind, she heard questions. What was she doing? How could she give in to his charms with such ease? Where would this lead? Yet, at the moment, they were just words and meant nothing. She couldn't stop—not now. She didn't even want to.

Above her, Brett groaned with each deep stroke, and his pounding movements reverberated all through her body, each delivering an incredible wave of warmth. The tender way he'd kissed her before had been perfect, and the hard way he made love to her now felt just as right. How could this be? How could this man love her so well?

His words still played in her mind. *Because now I love you.* The memory only served to make her feel that much closer to him, that much more complete in his arms. Could it be? Could he truly be in love with her?

"Oh," he moaned above her.

"Brett." She whispered his name, soft as a sigh, just to hear herself say it.

"I can't hold back."

She closed her eyes as he released his passion inside her, realizing for the first time that he hadn't used a condom, that he was inside her, flesh to flesh, and that in this grand and marvelous moment they were as connected as two human beings could be. As his strokes slowed, he lowered his head to her chest once more. She hugged him to her, tight and warm.

They lay silent on the table for a few minutes, the only sound that of their breathing. Darkness had fallen around them and a streetlamp outside created a grid of light through the window, falling serenely across the floor.

Then Summer's stomach growled, and Brett laughed.

"Did you work up an appetite?"

Their eyes met through the shadows and she gave him a smile. "I didn't eat dinner," she admitted. "I was on my way home from work when I stopped by."

"Well, I think the baby is hungry," he said playfully, rising off of her.

"I think you're right."

"Would he like a hot ham and Swiss? I went to the deli last night."

She sat up on the table. "Ham and Swiss would be fine," she said, then took the opportunity to broach a subject that had been on her mind for some time. "You know, I've noticed that you tend to call the baby 'he' a lot. Do you have insider information or something?" she teased.

"Nope," Brett said, moving to the refrigerator, "that's just what I think." He stopped and looked back at her, tilting his head. "Are you gonna ask the doctor about that before the baby's born?"

She shook her head. "No, I want it to be a surprise."

"*I* won't be surprised," he told her with the confident air she'd first noticed about him. "It's definitely a boy."

She playfully scoffed at his sureness and hopped down from the table, amazed at how natural it felt to move naked around his kitchen. It was nice, easy. It didn't feel dirty or weird or any of the things she might have imagined. Making love on the kitchen table—definitely a first for her—hadn't felt odd, either. With Brett, everything always felt normal, and right. She loved that...and she hated it, too. So she just wouldn't think about it right now. For now, complete surrender seemed the only sensible way to go.

After they'd downed a couple of sandwiches and two large glasses of milk, they curled up on Brett's couch in a blanket. A little while later, Summer's stomach growled again, and they exchanged amused glances.

"He's a hungry little guy," Brett remarked.

"Dessert?" she asked hopefully. She *had* noticed her appetite increasing lately.

"My dessert provisions are pretty depleted," he said, rolling out from under her. "But I'll see what I can come up with."

A minute later he returned with a small bowl of strawberries, offering it to Summer with optimistic eyes. "Will these do?"

"Yummy," she said, taking the bowl.

Sitting up on the couch, Summer used two fingers to daintily extract and eat a strawberry, aware the entire time that Brett watched her. The cover had fallen away, baring her to the waist. She'd started out feeling hungry, but now she felt sexy instead.

"Do that again," he said, his voice unusually deep.

"Do what again?"

"Eat another strawberry."

Biting her lip, Summer picked another berry from the dish and bit into it. This time, cool, sticky juice ran down her chin. She glanced at Brett, but he was already leaning toward her. He gently licked the juice away, then pulled back, and the heat in his gaze made Summer surge with want beneath the blanket.

Soon they were feeding each other, and not long after that the strawberries weren't even making it to their mouths. Brett raked a strawberry across Summer's breast, squeezing the fragrant juice onto her nipple, then licking it off with the tip of his tongue.

"Ooh..." She hadn't meant for the sound to escape her, but it did.

Tantalized, Summer experimented by squeezing one of the red berries over *his* nipple, then flicking her tongue over the juice to lick it off. "Mmm..." he breathed above her.

Within moments, the clear pink juice ran down their stomachs and over their chests, and was licked and kissed away. Summer didn't think she'd ever experienced anything so sensual in her life. She pulled in her breath when Brett dragged a juicy strawberry up the flesh between her thighs, then dipped down to lick the juice away from there, as well.

"You're delicious," he told her, at once playful and serious as he moved back up beside her on the couch.

Summer bit her lip, remembering the erotic delights he'd bestowed there earlier. He'd done it the first time they'd made love, too, and it had seemed to her like the ultimate gift—no taking, all giving. She'd understood in those delectable moments that it had been all about her, all about his desire to bring her pleasure.

Now, despite all the conflicting emotions inside her, Summer wanted to return the gift, wanted to make it be all about *him*.

Her heart rose to her throat as she plucked a plump red strawberry from the dish on the coffee table and folded back the cover with her other hand. Brett followed her eyes to his thick arousal and, seeming to sense what was coming, drew in his breath.

Summer's own breathing turned ragged and short as she ran the berry over the length of him, squeezing out the juice with her fingertips, before slowly lowering her head, taking him into her mouth.

Her heart beat like wild as she heard his trembling sighs above, and she marveled at having the ability to take him to the heights of ecstacy.

When she raised her head and their eyes met, nothing soft or gentle rested in his gaze—it was all fire. Suddenly he hauled her up against him, hard and fast and tight, and their sticky bodies pressed together and he found his way inside her. Moments later, Summer felt those same, familiar bursting flashes of energy and heat taking hold of her, wringing her body of sense and decision, and just as the wondrous waves subsided, it was happening for Brett, too. "Ah, Summer. I love you, Summer."

Even spent and sated as she was, Summer found it hard to relax after the intimacy they'd just shared. Every part of her being roared with energy, and her skin wouldn't stop tingling. "Brett, can I tell you something?" she whispered, bitten with the surprising urge to confide in him.

"Anything," he breathed back.

She took a deep breath before speaking. "I never did that before."

She didn't need to tell him what she was talking about, although he looked positively amazed. "Really?"

She nodded.

"Oh God," he said, lifting a hand to her cheek. "You are so sweet, honey. So perfect."

The endearments washed over her like soft silk—smooth and light and incredible.

"Why," he asked gently then, "did you do it for *me*?"

The question took Summer's breath away. She hadn't expected it and she didn't know the answer—or maybe she did, deep down inside. It lurked like a serpent beneath the water's surface, something she couldn't quite see and maybe didn't want to. "I...don't know," she told him. "It just..."

"What?"

"Felt right."

His warm sigh and sweet embrace enveloped her, and she fell asleep in his arms, feeling the same way she always felt with Brett. Happy, but afraid to feel that way.

WAKING UP STICKY, Brett prodded Summer into the shower, where they washed each other clean and made love once more beneath the warm spray.

Lying in bed a little while later, he found himself running his hand over her skin—her arm, shoulder, breast. "You're like satin," he whispered sleepily. When his palm slid smoothly over the ever-so-slight rise in her belly, he stopped and let it rest there. He knew it was too soon to feel anything moving, yet still it amazed him to think that his baby was inside her, right there.

She glanced down at his hand through the darkness. "All my clothes are getting tight," she said. "I thought

I'd have more time before that happened, but the doctor warned me that since I'm petite, I might start showing earlier. I'm starting to feel fat."

"It's not fat," he told her. "It's the baby."

He shifted his gaze from his hand to her face to see her staring toward the ceiling now, eyes half-open. "I know, but I've always been very...conscious of my body, of how I look. Too many Barbie dolls growing up, I guess." She turned her eyes to him. "I don't like the idea of getting big."

Brett's heart swelled with all the love he felt for her in that moment. The honesty that poured from her both touched and saddened him, and he wanted to take away all her worries.

"You're beautiful, Summer," he told her. "And the baby growing inside you is beautiful, too." He leaned over and lowered a kiss to her cheek, and they said no more before drifting into sleep.

SUMMER AWOKE the next morning to the sounds and scents of frying bacon wafting from the kitchen. Pale sunlight shone across the bedroom. It was the first time she'd seen the room in the light and she studied it. There was a dresser and chest of drawers against the far wall and a clothes hamper in one corner, currently overflowing. Above her rose the cathedral ceiling he'd told her about, and a fan turned in slow circles overhead.

Memories of the previous evening came back, striking hard and fast, making her recall...everything. She'd made love to him. More than that. She'd made wild, wonderful, terrible love to him. The very recollection was draining and made her think for a moment, *no, that couldn't have happened, not to me.* But she knew it *had* happened—she'd experienced some of the most intense moments of her life last night with Brett. She'd thought making love to him the first time was powerful, yet it was nothing compared to the completeness and intimacy they'd shared last evening.

Then the panic filled her, the same panic as always—there was no pushing it down. What had she done? Even if it *was* wonderful, what had she let happen here? Now he was in the kitchen cooking her breakfast, and soon she'd see his sweet, crooked smile and hear his warm, deep voice, and she'd instantly be buried again by wanting him.

No, no, no. You need control, she told herself. *Get it back! Now!*

What should she do? *Get up, put your clothes on, and go. Thank him for a wonderful evening, but tell him that you're late for a meeting or something.* She glanced at the clock. It was after nine. Damn, she remembered then it was Saturday. Now what excuse could she use to get out of his apartment?

An unfamiliar voice from somewhere inside whispered to her. *Don't go. Stay. Let him love you. Let him make you happy.*

Yet the same old arguments arose fresh in her mind. She didn't want to share her life, or her decisions, with anyone, let alone a man who made her feel so horribly weak and helpless inside. And even if she was forced to share her baby with him, she wanted to keep their contact as brief as possible.

The fact was, she still didn't really know this guy. She knew things *about* him. She knew where he worked and where he lived, and she knew how good he was in bed. She even knew he could be undeniably sweet. But those weren't reasons enough to suddenly give up your independence and offer to share your entire life with a man. Were they?

Brett stuck his head in the room. Summer flinched, but he didn't seem to notice. "Hey, sleepy head," he said. Same adorable grin as always, burying her.

"Um...hey." She felt numb. Why did he have to look so good to her, even with messy morning hair, wearing a rumpled T-shirt and gym shorts? Why did the very sight of him twist her stomach into adolescent knots?

"How do you like your eggs?"

"Over easy," she replied. Drat, that meant she had to stay at least through breakfast. And God only knew what would happen after that.

"Did I prove it?" he asked cheerfully.

"Huh? Prove what?"

"Did I prove we were good together?"

She swallowed. He was coming at her with this already? "Well...yes, I can't deny that, Brett. But—"

Summer was interrupted by a knock at the door that turned Brett's head. "Who could that be?" he muttered, then looked back to Summer. "Um, grab a T-shirt out of the dresser if you want. I'll get rid of whoever it is."

Summer scurried from the bed, anxious to cover her nakedness, and just as anxious to finish what she'd been saying. Why did someone have to arrive *now*?

She found a large gray T-shirt with a faded Ohio State logo on the front, along with a pair of drawstring shorts. She put them both on, thinking, *please let whoever's at the door go away, and please let me get through this as quickly as possible.* She would just have to tell him, yes, they were good together, but no, she wasn't ready to marry him or even allow him an important space in her life. Things were just too perfectly in place for her as they were, and the last ten years of her existence had been spent making them that way. She wasn't going to let anyone mess that up.

"Hey, guys, what's going on?" Brett said happily in the other room. This did not exactly sound to Summer like getting-rid-of tactics.

A woman's voice answered. "We're setting off for a day of outlet malls and thought we'd see if you wanted to come."

"Or, if you'd prefer," *another* female voice said, "the guys are taking the kids to the zoo."

"Uh...wow," Brett said, "your timing's not so hot. Ever think of calling first?"

A *third* woman replied. "I told her that. But she insisted on just stopping by."

God, how many people were out there? Summer wondered, lowering herself onto the bed.

Then an undeniably weighty pause seemed to fill the air until the first woman finally spoke again. "Uh-oh."

"Uh-oh what?" the second woman asked.

"Uh-oh, a bra," the first replied.

"Oops," said the second.

Oh God! Summer held in her gasp, but she wanted to die! All her clothes, stripped hurriedly from her body last night, still lay in a heap on the kitchen floor. She gripped nervously at the mattress on either side of her. *Make them go away,* she willed him. *Whoever they are, make them go away.*

One of them giggled as another one spoke. "Guess that's what you meant by bad timing."

Brett's voice dropped to a whisper. "For God's sake, you guys wanna keep it down?"

More feminine giggles echoed, followed by a muttered, "Damn. Hi, Mom," from Brett. "Uh, why didn't you guys tell me Mom was here?"

Hi, *Mom?* Summer thought. *Oh no! This couldn't be happening! It really, really couldn't!*

"Nice to see you, too," his mother said sarcastically.

"I'm just a little surprised," he replied, sounding sheepish.

"There's a girl here, Mom," one of the females said in a too-loud whisper. Which cleared up one mystery: they were Brett's sisters. But who could think about that now?

One of them cleared her throat dramatically and all went silent in the other room. Summer imagined them all standing there gaping at her bra, not to mention her panties, hosiery, blouse and suit. *Oh God, this was bad. Really bad.* She wanted to crawl under the bed and never come out.

"See, Susan, I told you we should have called," his mother said.

"So, is it serious, or just…one of those things?"

"Do we get to meet her?"

"You guys, leave him alone. The poor woman's probably in there cowering."

Well, they'd hit that one on the head, Summer thought.

"We're sorry, dear," his mother apologized. "We'll go and leave you be."

"No," he suddenly said, to Summer's immediate and intense distress.

No? No…? What the hell was he thinking?

"Since you ask," he said, "I do want you to meet her."

Summer sucked in her breath. *He wanted them to meet her? Now? Like this?*

At first she was sure she must have misheard him, because he couldn't possibly have said that. But he had. Had he completely lost his mind?

"Cool," one of his sisters replied.

"And she's probably gonna kill me for this," he told them, "since it's hardly ideal timing."

Kill, Summer thought, was a mild term for what she intended to do to Brett.

"But you really should meet her," he continued.

"We should?"

They should?

"Summer," he called merrily. "Don't kill me, honey, but will you come say hi?"

She couldn't believe this. Was he serious or was this some cruel practical joke? And did he have to sound so *normal* about it, like this was only some minor inconvenience and not the most tragic, humiliating moment of her life?

"Too late," she replied from the bedroom. "I *am* going to kill you. And it's going to be slow. There will be torture involved."

"I want you to meet my mom and my sisters," he said just as cheerfully as if she hadn't replied.

"Brett," she called, feeling desperate and already quite mortified enough. "You can't be serious about this. You really can't."

"Don't be embarrassed," he said. As if it were that simple, as if she could just snap her fingers and not want to crawl in a hole anymore.

"We're really very nice," one of the sisters called.

And she *did* sound nice, but that made no difference. Summer was wearing his clothes, for God's sake, and they were all standing out there looking at her intimate apparel.

"Please, Summer," he begged. "You may as well. They're not gonna go away and the bathroom window is too small for you to crawl through."

Summer wanted to explode. What was she supposed to do? At this point, it seemed a no-win situation. If she went out there, it would be humiliating. As it was, she was already humiliated. All she knew was that she really *was* going to kill Brett! And she was going to make sure he suffered first!

Gathering every ounce of her courage, Summer rose from the bed and timidly poked her head around through the wide doorway.

Three women—all of them with dark brown hair like Brett's—stood with the older lady who she knew was Brett's mother.

"Hi," she whispered. Then she looked to Brett with narrowed eyes. "You're a dead man," she said through clenched teeth.

He ignored her threat, which infuriated her all the more. "Mom, Brenda, Jackie, Susan," he said, "meet Summer, the woman I'm going to marry."

All the air left Summer's lungs.

She felt her mouth drop open, and reached to clutch at the doorway before she fainted.

He hadn't just said that, had he? *Oh God, he had!* "*Brett!*" she hissed sharply in protest, but no one even heard her.

"Oh wow, that's great!"

"Baby brother, I'm so happy for you!"

"Why didn't you tell us?"

"This is wonderful!"

"A wedding! I *love* weddings!"

Susan and Jackie rushed toward Summer, hugging her, and she thought she might just collapse in their arms.

"It's about time we got him married off," Jackie said.

"Welcome to the family," sang Susan.

Summer stood dumbfounded before them. This wasn't her, not in-control Summer Avery. Couldn't be. She'd clearly entered someone else's body. She rolled her eyes at the thought—if only it were that simple.

"I'm glad you're happy," Brett said to his family then, "because there's more."

Everyone paused and turned to look at him.

"More?" they said in unison.

Oh no. Summer could hear it coming.

"We're having a baby!" he announced before she could make a move to stop him.

Summer was pretty sure she really would pass out soon, but something kept her standing, probably the numerous embraces that came between the wide-eyed grins and enthusiastic congratulations that surrounded her on all sides.

"Well then," Jackie finally said, "we'll have to work fast!"

"Fast?" Summer murmured.

"On the wedding," Susan replied. "But don't worry. All three of us were married in the last seven years— bam, bam, bam, one after the other—so we're expert planners and we've got connections all over town."

"We can help with everything!" Jackie gushed. "It'll be wonderful!"

Before Summer could even catch her breath, Brett's mother, an elegant yet friendly looking woman who wore her silver-gray hair in a short, tidy style, moved in for her first hug. "Welcome to the family, dear. I'm very happy for you both."

Summer tried to force a smile, since she certainly couldn't get out any words.

Only then did she notice that Brenda still stood just inside the door and had offered no congratulations or any of the hugs the rest of them seemed so fond of giving. Maybe she sensed Summer's hesitance. Or maybe she was shier than her sisters. Well, whatever the reason, Summer had a lot more to worry about right now, like how to get out of this...and how to kill Brett in the slowest, most painful way possible.

Say no, she commanded herself. *Say no to all of this. Do it right now, don't let it go any further.*

But Brett's two sisters and mother were still gathered around her, one of them draping an arm around Summer's shoulder as if they'd known each other forever. They were already discussing colors for the wedding— someone suggested plum—and it was so obvious that Brett was their pride and joy that, for some reason, Summer just couldn't do it. She just couldn't tell them that she wouldn't marry him.

A part of her felt as desperate as ever, like she wanted to escape from the nearest window as Brett had suggested or perhaps tunnel her way down to Mrs. Greenbaum's below—anything to get out of this somehow.

Yet deep down inside, another part of her was filled with elation at the idea of having Brett every day for the rest of her life. She shuddered at the startling revelation, again worrying that she might faint, but it was true.

After Brett finally herded the family out of the apartment with a promise that they'd both come over for dinner the following night to start planning the wedding, he shut the door and calmly turned to face Summer.

Their eyes met, hers steeled and ready.

She enunciated carefully. "You are dead," she said, taking a step toward him.

"I know, I know... It was a dirty thing of me to do, but—"

"Say your prayers," she told him, "because I'm about to rip you limb from limb." She drew nearer still.

He shook his head in supposed regret. "Summer, honey, I know it was rotten of me—"

"Rotten doesn't begin to describe what it was." He was within her reach now.

"But I know we'll look back on this someday and laugh," he added, "which is why you should forgive me."

"Forgive you? *Forgive you?* No way in hell."

Brett grabbed her then, drawing her into his arms and lowering a long, heat-filled kiss to her acceptant lips. Oh damn it, she wanted to push him away. She wanted to beat him to a pulp. At the very least, she wanted to walk out on him.

Yet she couldn't do any of those things. She could only kiss him, kiss him, kiss him. As always, she could only kiss him, until her head felt like it was spinning and her blood seemed charged with electricity.

When he finally pulled back long enough for Summer to take a breath and look into his intoxicating blue eyes, he was smiling. "This is gonna be great, Summer. You'll see."

"What's gonna be great?" she snapped.

"Getting married."

"Getting *married*," she repeated belligerently. "What on *earth* makes you think that we're getting *married*?"

He raised his eyebrows and deepened his grin. "You didn't say no."

5

SUMMER AND BRETT STOOD on his parents' front porch. Summer wore a loose-fitting sundress in an attempt to hide her slightly bulging belly, and also with the thought of trying to project some sunny, happy, friendly image that she wanted his family to have of her—the woman who was about to have their only son's baby. She didn't think she'd ever been so nervous in her life.

"Ready?" Brett asked with a smile as he rang the doorbell.

"No," she said, but he only laughed and grabbed her hand in his easy, adoring way. Although she really wanted to kill him, and still couldn't believe she was going along with this, something kept her going through the motions.

Without warning, Summer reached to lift the hair on both sides of her face. "Are the earrings too much?" They were large, bright sunflowers, and it suddenly dawned on her that perhaps she'd taken the sunny, happy, friendly thing a little too far.

He shook his head. "They're fine. I like 'em."

They'd spent the day and a half since the embarrassing—not to mention life-changing—scene at Brett's apartment together. They hadn't done anything in particular, just the regular things people did: eating, talking, picking up a new tie for Brett at Stafford's for a presentation he had to make on Tuesday, as well as buying the sundress Summer now wore, and on Saturday night he'd taken her to a movie.

So it was as if they were dating, she thought as she stood there waiting at the door. Which would make them like normal people, with normal lives. Summer let the comforting idea settle around her and give her courage. After all, people who dated met each other's parents all the time, right? So this was all okay—they were sensible, regular, *normal* people.

Except for one thing. *He'd tricked her into saying she'd marry him.*

Possibly the most shocking part of this was that Summer didn't seem to be protesting any longer. She wasn't sure why or what could have come over her, but every time she considered telling him there was no way in hell she'd walk down an aisle with him, especially after the way he'd gone about gaining her capitulation, she couldn't do it. She'd look at him and find him smiling at her, his eyes shining, or he'd squeeze her hand or lean over and kiss her on the cheek, and it would somehow be enough to lull her into keeping silent.

So now she stood here, ready to actually meet his family and plan a wedding with them. She shook her head at the sheer insanity of it.

Feeling panicky and just a little irrational, Summer reached up and quickly removed both earrings. "Take these," she said, holding them out to Brett.

"Thanks, but they're really not my style."

She made an impatient face. "I didn't bring a purse. Can you keep them in your pocket for me?"

"Summer, they look fine. Honest."

Just then the door before her burst open with a great whoosh of air. A balding, slightly overweight man of around sixty stood on the other side, beaming at her. He wore two oven mitts with cat faces on them. "Sorry it took so long for me to get to the door. Lois and I were fighting to get that huge lasagna tray she uses out of the oven. Too big for one person to handle, if you can believe that. But she says with a crowd our size, and a belly like this one—" he patted his stomach "—nothing else is big enough. You must be Summer. I'm Brett's dad, Stanley, and I'm thrilled to meet you. Come on in." He reached for her hand, stopping to laugh when he realized he still wore the oven mitts, and his eyes fell on the two sunflower earrings still in Summer's outstretched palm. "Why, thanks," he said without missing a beat, "but you didn't have to bring me a present. Do you think they'll clash with my hair?" He winked at her, and she and Brett exchanged glances, Brett shrugging as if to say, *I have no idea where the guy gets his sense of humor.*

In the blink of an eye, Summer had seen why Brett's father meant so much to him. And as much as she might hate to admit it, she also suddenly understood why it was so important to Brett for *his* child to have a father. The knowledge twisted her stomach, for it seemed to go one step further to support the fact that this was really happening, that they were moving full steam ahead with this let's-get-married-and-be-a-family thing.

Summer went through the same nervous embarrassment as Brett's dad ushered her enthusiastically into the dining room, mitts still in place. "Nice look, Dad," Brett's sister Susan said wryly from the table where she sat with Jackie, poring over bridal magazines. Her expression brightened as she flipped her long, straight hair over her shoulder. "Hi, Summer. Hope you're ready to be bombarded with about a hundred decisions."

Summer drew in her breath. As if she wasn't being

bombarded enough already. *Dear God, what was she even doing here?* she thought as she smiled at Susan.

Brett's mother appeared in the doorway that led from the kitchen. "Don't let her scare you, Summer. It may all seem a little overwhelming at first, but we're here to help out."

"That's good," she finally managed to reply, "because I have a feeling I'm going to need all the help I can get." After all, most women spent years daydreaming about their wedding, but not Summer. She hadn't the first idea what was involved, and she had more than a few doubts that any of this should be happening at all.

Behind her, Brett cleared his throat, and she felt the pleasant warmth of his hand at the small of her back. "Let's not forget the groom, guys," he said. Even without looking at him, she sensed his grin. "Don't I get a say in any of this?"

Susan and Jackie exchanged a playful look before Susan said, "Brett, you can barely match your socks in the morning."

Summer knew his sister was just teasing him—she'd seen him in a suit enough times to know he had impeccable taste in clothing—but nevertheless Brett said, "Hey, I resent that."

"Maybe you should run along with Dad," Jackie suggested, attempting to shoo the men from the room, "and find something manly to do while we figure all this out."

"And let you girls eat up all my lasagna?" their father replied. "I don't think so. Sit down, Brett. Let's show these womenfolk what we're made of. We've got a wedding to plan."

It turned out that Jackie and Susan were the only sisters present. Someone mentioned that Brett's oldest sister, Brenda, had previous plans with her husband's family. Jackie and Susan both had families of their own, too, yet their husbands had opted out of the wedding planning session, as well—understandably enough—and taken the kids to a movie.

Summer couldn't quit wondering what all these very nice people must think of her, this stranger whom they'd practically found in their brother's or son's bed, this woman who was suddenly going to have his baby. Nonetheless, their enthusiasm and kindness put her more at ease than she'd have imagined possible, and after dinner, the wedding work began.

Before the night was done, a multitude of decisions had been made, and Summer couldn't believe how surreal it all seemed, how *unreal*. To her unqualified disbelief, she actually seemed to be letting this wedding be arranged.

When the evening concluded with Brett's father putting an old record on a turntable—Frank Sinatra singing "I've Got You Under My Skin"—and whisking his wife into his arms for an impromptu dance, Summer watched in awe, thinking, *What wonderful people and what a wonderful love they share, still finding joy in each other's arms even all these years later.* After everything else she'd experienced tonight, it left her a little breathless. Could it be like that for her and Brett? Could they find themselves some thirty or forty years from now still in love, still wanting to share dances and laughter? Could they be surrounded by their children, all grown and happy, all products of the love they gave each other?

Strangely, she shuddered at the thought. It seemed too good to be true, too long a road to believe two people could travel together with too many obstacles to overcome along the way. Yet then Brett's hand found her elbow, and as she looked up into his warm blue eyes, he said, "Care to dance?"

Summer felt a little weak with the romance of it all. "Um, yes."

Brett slid his arms around her, the sensation of his body against hers as sweet and hot as ever as he turned her slowly around the dining room. His parents danced alongside them and his sisters whispered too loudly about how cute they were together, and for a few magical minutes, Summer understood completely why she hadn't said no to any of this. She wanted desperately to hang on to her control, yet this was all too perfect to fight. She didn't know how she'd feel tomorrow, but for right now, right this moment, she *believed*...she believed they could have it all.

A FEW DAYS LATER, Summer stood before a large mirror, yards of white satin billowing around her. "Oh, that looks great on you!" Susan said, her blue eyes wide in the mirror behind Summer. "I like it so much better than the last one."

Summer smiled her appreciation. Susan, the most outgoing and fun-loving of Brett's three sisters, had quickly become her favorite.

Standing next to Susan, Jackie nodded, her neatly bobbed hair bouncing with each movement of her head. "She's right. It really suits you." As the middle sister, Jackie seemed a little more subdued than Susan, but Summer had found her friendly and sincere, and had soon discovered herself trusting Jackie's opinion.

"Not too...floofy and girlish?" Summer asked. The high-necked, sleeveless bodice was covered in lace, dropping to a loose V at the waist and the satin skirt below flowed in all directions. The look appealed to her,

The Harlequin Reader Service® — Here's how it works:

Accepting your 2 free books and gift places you under no obligation to buy anything. You may keep the books and gift and return the shipping statement marked "cancel." If you do not cancel, about a month later we'll send you 4 additional novels and bill you just $3.34 each in the U.S., or $3.80 each in Canada, plus 25¢ shipping & handling per book and applicable taxes if any.* That's the complete price and — compared to cover prices of $3.99 each in the U.S. and $4.50 each in Canada — it's quite a bargain! You may cancel at any time, but if you choose to continue, every month we'll send you 4 more books, which you may either purchase at the discount price or return to us and cancel your subscription.

*Terms and prices subject to change without notice. Sales tax applicable in N.Y. Canadian residents will be charged applicable provincial taxes and GST.

If offer card is missing write to: Harlequin Reader Service, 3010 Walden Ave., P.O. Box 1867, Buffalo NY 14240-1867

BUSINESS REPLY MAIL

FIRST-CLASS MAIL   PERMIT NO. 717   BUFFALO, NY

POSTAGE WILL BE PAID BY ADDRESSEE

HARLEQUIN READER SERVICE
3010 WALDEN AVE
PO BOX 1867
BUFFALO NY 14240-9952

NO POSTAGE
NECESSARY
IF MAILED
IN THE
UNITED STATES

but her fashion expertise didn't extend to selecting her own bridal gown with confidence.

"It's not girlish at all," Jackie said. "In fact, I think it's sophisticated yet somewhat simple, too. Simple but elegant is always a smart choice."

"Besides," Susan said, beaming, "it's your wedding! It's okay to be girlish or sophisticated or whatever you want to be!"

Summer laughed at Susan's fun view of things. As she'd figured out the other night at Brett's parents' house, having Susan and Jackie around made all of this much easier than she could have envisioned.

Just then, Tina burst through the door behind them wearing blue jeans, a stylish halter top and a pair of tiny, octagonal sunglasses, which she whipped off as she drew to a stop. "Sorry I'm late. Oh my God, you look fab!" she said, her eyes wide.

"You really like it?" Even though Summer trusted Jackie's and Susan's opinions, Tina *did* have a way with fashion, both on the job and personally.

Her friend nodded. "In fact, if you don't buy it, I will. I know, I know," she added with a smile, "I don't have a groom, but..."

"Take it from me, you never know when one will show up when you least expect it," Summer said, making everyone laugh.

In the midst of the shared humor, Summer caught sight of Brenda standing across the bridal shop, chatting with one of the women who worked there. Just as she had the morning at Brett's apartment when Summer had first met them all, Brenda seemed disinterested in any of this. Was it just Summer or did Brenda not like her? Oh, she'd been polite enough, and at moments had even gone so far as to seem friendly, yet compared to Jackie

and Susan, Brenda seemed...*unenthusiastic* about the
wedding, to say the least.

More than once today, Summer wondered why
Brenda had decided to come along in the first place if
she wasn't going to take part in what they were doing.

Thinking of the old saying about flies and honey,
Summer decided to take the first step in mending whatever was wrong between them. "Would you come tell
me what you think of this dress?" She smiled boldly.

She couldn't read Brenda's face as she made her way
across the room, her short, dark hair curved over her
cheeks in a way that made her emotions even harder to
detect, but when she arrived, she studied the dress in silence for a moment, then returned Summer's smile. The
expression didn't quite reach her eyes, but Summer figured she'd take what she could get for now. "I like it,"
Brenda said of the dress. "It becomes you."

"Thank you," Summer replied, trying to sound very
warm and appreciative. She would win Brenda over yet.

Turning her gaze back to the mirror, Summer caught
her breath at the sight of herself in a wedding gown.
Things had moved ahead so quickly, a bit *too* quickly.
One minute she'd been shanghaied into accepting
Brett's proposal, the next his family had started planning their huge, gala, whirlwind wedding. She wanted
to believe it had all happened before she could even
think about putting a stop to it, but that wasn't true. She
had thought about it. She spent almost every second of
every day now thinking about ending the charade, and
yet she still didn't. Now here she stood, taking on the
last role she'd ever expected to find herself in—the
blushing bride-to-be—and trying desperately to win
over a reluctant family member, at that.

The saleslady who'd been helping them suddenly ar-rived at her side. "How do you like the gown?"

"She loves it!" Susan answered for her. "It's the best one yet."

Summer smiled, admitting, "It *is* lovely."

The genteel yet sprightly lady fished a strand of pearls out of her jacket pocket and reached up to hook them around Summer's neck. From the other pocket, she pro-duced a pair of dainty white lace wrist gloves. "Try these," she said.

Summer slipped on the gloves, inwardly delighted at the way they made her ensemble look somehow prim yet...lively. She thought of the prim part as her original self, and of the lively part as the new self she'd discov-ered since meeting Brett.

Just as quickly, she wondered at her own reaction, to the gloves and to the image she'd let them create in her mind. Was she really getting all caught up in this? In a wedding? In marrying Brett? Was it all this simple? Or, again, had she let this get outrageously out of hand?

She sighed, trying to make sense of it all. In one way, it felt magical—everything involving Brett seemed to have a horribly wonderful effect on her—and yet in an-other way, she still harbored the same old doubts.

She cared for Brett—she knew that now and didn't even try to delude herself into thinking differently—but she was about to commit her *life* to him. In so doing, she was agreeing to let someone else share in all the deci-sions she made from this point forward, for the baby and for herself.

"Where's Brett today, anyway?" Jackie asked, cutting in on Summer's negative thoughts.

"He's moving some stuff into my house," Summer re-plied, though even as she spoke the words, they nearly caught in her throat. *He was moving things into her house! Their lives were becoming one!* It was almost too much to take.

Of course, his sisters and mother made the wedding part easy. With their help the other night, plans for the event were practically finalized. And now, as her maid of honor, Tina had gotten involved, too.

"How do you feel about pale yellow?" Tina asked just then, approaching from behind with a refined-looking bridesmaid's dress dangling from a hanger in front of her.

"Actually," Summer said, "I like it a lot." The buttery shade made Summer think of springtime and sunshine. "But since you guys will be the ones wearing them, what do *you* think?"

"I love it," Jackie replied immediately, "and I'd be very happy wearing that dress. It's a style that someone of any age could feel good in."

Susan nodded her approval, too, although Brenda had already faded from the conversation. But under the circumstances, input from three out of four of her attendants seemed good enough to Summer.

"How about yellow roses?" Susan suggested. "Wouldn't that be stunning?"

"Simple but elegant," Jackie said once more, raising her eyebrows as if to say *This is all coming together*.

"And the gloves make that dress, by the way," Tina chimed in.

"What do you think, Summer?" Susan prodded.

Hmm, Summer thought. The yellow dresses with matching roses, the dainty gloves and the gown she wore... "I think it all sounds...very promising," she said, an image of the wedding really forming in her mind for the first time.

With the help of Brett's family, Summer had already arranged for the church on a date in late July, the cocktail reception afterward and the honeymoon suite at the Cincinnatian, the grand refurbished hotel downtown.

All that had led to honeymoon planning, as well. Brett had wanted to take her to Hawaii for a week, but that's where Summer had put her foot down—there was no way he was getting her into a bathing suit right now. She'd suggested they do something relaxing instead, like renting a cabin in the mountains, and he hadn't argued. She supposed he realized how lucky he was that she hadn't called this whole thing off yet.

Behind her, Brett's mother appeared. "Okay, girls, I just spoke with the caterer. He had to move our appointment to three o'clock, so we'll need to wrap this up soon."

At this, Summer again studied the dress she wore, trying to make a final decision, just as Brett's mother lifted her hand to her chest, apparently breathless. "Oh Summer, my dear, that dress is...divine."

"She's right, Summer," Susan said.

"Way gorgeous," Tina added.

Summer couldn't deny that it was exquisite, and the slightly loose cut didn't even make her look pregnant— at least not yet. If she was actually doing this, actually getting married, she didn't think she could find a lovelier gown to do it in. "I'll take it," she said, letting a smile find her lips.

Susan and Jackie both practically cheered as the bridal-salon lady whisked a tape measure from her pocket and moved in to start planning alterations.

STANDING BEFORE THE MIRROR, Brett turned one way, then another. He thought the simple black tux looked good, but he wasn't well versed in formal wear. He'd *worn* plenty of it before, in other guys' weddings, yet he'd never had occasion to actually *select* it. And it was still a bit hard to fathom that he would soon be having a wedding of his own. Nonetheless, Summer had picked out her dress a week ago, and he'd received strict instructions from his sisters that he was to choose a tux today, no ifs, ands or buts.

He looked at himself grinning into the mirror like some kind of goofball. Damn, he was overjoyed. All day, all night, all the time, he couldn't quit being happy. He couldn't get used to the idea that he was actually getting to marry Summer! Of course, in the end, he hadn't exactly gone about securing her acceptance in the most aboveboard way, but he couldn't regret what he'd done. He knew in his heart that the wedding was right, and that they'd be happy.

Behind him, Brenda approached. His other two sisters were busy with Summer at the florist's this afternoon, so Brenda had come along to help him. "What do you think?" he asked, taking hold of his lapels and smiling at her in the mirror.

"Looks good," she said, yet behind her smile, the expression in her brown gaze was clearly hollow.

What was with her, anyway? She hadn't been herself lately, but Brett refused to let it infringe on his happiness. He felt too good to let anything bring him down.

"So," she asked, "why the big, silly grin?"

He cast her a playful scowl in the mirror, then replied, "Because a few months ago I was a single guy, alone, with no real prospects for changing that anytime soon, and now, suddenly, I'm gonna be a husband and a father. Isn't that amazing?"

To his annoyance, she didn't return his smile this

time. In fact, she actually wore a frown. "Since you mention it, Brett..."

"Yeah?" He sensed something bad here.

"All this has...happened awfully quick."

He didn't like her worried tone. "So?"

"So...are you sure about marrying her?"

Brett couldn't have been more stunned. As his oldest sibling, Brenda had always been a little protective, but he'd never expected her to rain on his wedding. "Of course I'm sure."

"You love her then?"

He turned from the mirror to face her. "Hell yes, I love her. Why would you think I didn't love her?"

"Brett, I just want to make sure you're not rushing into anything, that's all."

"Just because it happened fast," he explained, "doesn't mean I'm rushing."

Her voice dropped dramatically. "Is this why you gave up Paris?"

The question shocked him almost as much as the first one had. He sighed, not really wanting to go into this. No one else in the family had brought it up yet and he'd thought—hoped—that maybe no one would.

Now that she'd asked, though, he'd be honest with her. "Yeah. It is."

"Oh, Brett." She gave her head a disdainful shake.

"What?" he snapped.

"How could you give up Paris?" She whispered it as if he'd given up a child or something. Which, he thought ironically, was exactly what he *hadn't* done.

"I'm getting married and having a baby," he told her. "What else would I do?"

"But you were so excited," she reminded him. "You wanted to work on that project so badly."

Yes, he had. It had been a dream come true, an event that would have altered the course of his life and sent him in new directions...yet everything was different since then. Other events had changed his life and led him in *unexpected* new directions that were just as exciting, if not more so. How could she not understand his decision? How could she have expected him to do anything else?

"And now *this* is what I want," he told her pointedly, casting a glance of warning that said to drop the subject.

"THIS IS FROM SUSAN," Summer announced, reading the gift card. She sat in a large easy chair in the Fords' living room, surrounded by all of Brett's sisters and aunts. The only face from her "pre-Brett" days belonged to Tina. It was more than a little nerve-racking being the center of attention in a group of people who knew only that she'd gotten pregnant out of wedlock by Brett, but somehow Summer was holding herself together.

She pulled the lid off the box and extracted a beautiful pink silk chemise. A heart-shaped sachet covered in lace lay tucked into one corner of the pink tissue paper below. "Oh Susan," she breathed, "this is gorgeous!" The rest of the ladies oohed and ahhed accordingly.

"For the wedding night," Susan said, her pale blue eyes going typically wide and playful.

Summer blushed and polite giggles rippled across the room, and even in spite of her slight embarrassment, she couldn't help but appreciate the thought that had gone into her future sister-in-law's gift. Summer had expressed her concern over her appearance as the pregnancy progressed, and Susan had found something pretty that would de-accentuate that part of her body. "Thank you," she said warmly, meeting Susan's eyes.

Only one more gift to go, she thought, lifting the last pristinely wrapped box from its spot on the carpet. From Tina she'd gotten a ridiculously sexy but admittedly fun leopard print bra and panty set that she would likely save for later—after she had the baby—and from Jackie, a set of thick, beautifully monogrammed towels. From Brenda she'd received a waffle iron, along with the new knowledge that Brett loved homemade waffles. Yet even as Brenda had shared the information with a smile, Summer feared that deep down, Brenda still didn't approve of her or their marriage.

"Well, open it," Susan prodded, shaking Summer from her thoughts.

She pulled the attached card from the little envelope and announced that the gift was from Brett's mother. The message read, "Wishing you and Brett much happiness as you begin your new life together. Love, Mom."

Simple as it was, Summer's stomach twisted with emotion. *Love, Mom.* She would be part of a family now, a *real* family. She'd never had that before. Even with her own parents, she'd always felt a bit disassociated from their lives. Although they'd always been generous with their love, they'd been so much older and so deeply out of touch with people her age. And she'd never known what it was like to have brothers or sisters, anyone to share things with or laugh with. Warmth pooled inside her at the knowledge that she would get to experience all those things. She'd never thought that kind of stuff mattered...but maybe it did.

"*Well?*" Susan said, motioning toward the still unopened gift.

Summer flinched. "Sorry, I'm just...a little lost in thought."

Mrs. Ford, who had insisted Summer call her Lois,

paused from handing out hors d'oeuvres to step forward and pat her shoulder, smiling down on her with warm blue eyes the same shade as Brett's. "Perfectly understandable, my dear," she said. "So many changes happening so quickly."

Summer nodded appreciatively, then finally removed the white ribbon and opened the box. Inside, nestled in a bed of lace, were two long-stemmed crystal goblets. "For the wedding toast," Lois said as Summer held them up.

Then Summer realized that what lay underneath was more than just package dressing. She pulled it from the box to discover a robe made entirely of white lace. She'd never seen anything so exquisite. "For *after* the wedding," Lois added, and Summer smiled.

Beneath the robe lay a white linen handkerchief with thick ruffled edges, and embroidered in yellow across it were the words, *Summer and Brett* and the date of their wedding, which was fast approaching, as it was nearly June now.

Summer simply stared at the hankie, which struck her as delicate and lovely and...permanent. It meant acceptance. Maybe not by Brenda, but by the rest of them. Most members of Brett's family were happy that Brett was marrying her, bringing her into their lives. "And that," Lois said, "is for forever. Just to keep."

"I think," Summer said, "I'd like to carry it with me in the wedding."

Lois smiled, obviously moved at the suggestion. "That would be delightful, dear."

Summer went through the rest of the shower in a haze. Cake and punch and snacks filled the room with sweet scents, and Summer heard one of Brett's aunts happily remark that soon they'd be getting together again for a *baby* shower. My God, it was all happening so fast! It was almost enough to overwhelm her, yet when she returned to the pile of gifts and plucked out the embroidered hankie, she felt...well, as if she wasn't in this alone. She didn't remember ever having felt that way before, at least not since she'd become an adult. These people actually cared about her!

"Are you all right?"

She glanced up from the handkerchief to find Jackie at her elbow, her light brown eyes wide with concern. "Just feeling...a little emotional," Summer said with a slight nod.

Over the wedding? Over the baby? She waited for Jackie to ask, but she didn't. Instead, Brett's sister just smiled and gave her a reassuring hug. She'd never have dreamed she could feel so close to these people so quickly, yet that's what had happened.

"All right, what am I missing out on?" Susan asked, approaching. "A big hugfest?" She didn't even wait for an answer before giving Summer yet another loose embrace.

"It's just that...I never had any sisters," Summer told them.

"Well, you do now," Jackie said.

Summer felt silly being so emotional, but this meant more to her than they could possibly know. Besides having no sisters, she really had no close friends at all other than Tina, since she was always so focused on her work and much more outgoing in business than in social situations. Oh sure, she made small talk to other women in the office, but Tina was the only person she'd actually formed a real bond with, probably because they worked so closely together. Besides, Tina's bubbly personality was infectious. She had a way of bringing Summer out of her shell without her even knowing it, and now Brett's sisters were having the same effect on her.

A little while later, after most of the guests had departed and cleanup had begun, Lois pulled Summer into her bedroom. "Can I speak to you in private?"

Oh God, Summer thought, panicking. Was something wrong?

Maybe Summer had misread this whole situation. Maybe Lois really *wasn't* happy. Maybe she was going to scold Summer for getting pregnant or warn her to treat Brett right or something horrible and humiliating like that. As they sat down together on the divan at the end of the bed, Summer braced herself for the worst.

"Summer," Lois said, taking one of Summer's hands between hers, "Brett told me about how your parents passed away when you were a young girl."

"Oh." This surprised her a little, but she didn't mind.

"And I just wanted to tell you...that I'm very pleased with Brett's choice for a wife, and I hope you know you'll be as much a daughter to me as my own girls are."

Summer couldn't move then, or breathe. She swallowed, trying to hold back tears, but it didn't work—they fought their way out and trickled down her cheeks. She hadn't known anyone could *really* be like this. She'd been alone for so long that she hadn't imagined what she was missing by not having a family.

"There, there, dear," Lois said, patting her hand. "I didn't mean to make you cry."

Summer shook her head. "I'm just...so touched."

Lois smiled. A mother's smile. Something else Summer had missed. "I understand."

"Mom!" Susan called from somewhere in the house. "The bakery guy's on the phone. He wants to reschedule the last cake appointment."

Lois rose to her feet, but urged Summer to stay. "Take a few minutes for yourself, dear. There's nothing going on out there that the rest of us can't handle."

Still in tears, Summer nodded her appreciation and watched Brett's mother depart. Then she closed her eyes and leaned her head back.

Quit crying, she thought. *Pull yourself together. Whatever happened to staying in control?* Must have gone the way of the dinosaurs, since she hadn't had any control over anything in weeks. And if she was truthful with herself, she was beginning to wonder if it even mattered. She didn't find herself missing it nearly as much as she might have expected.

"Hey there, why the tears?"

Summer opened her eyes and looked toward the doorway to see Brett. He came toward her, blue eyes brimming with concern. "What are you doing here?" she asked, sniffling.

"I stopped by to help you get the presents home. But I sure didn't expect to find my beautiful fiancée crying. What gives?"

Summer just shook her head, still not ready to talk. First his mother being so sweet, now him, too, the man she was going to marry... She simply couldn't get over it all.

When she didn't answer, but only started crying harder, Brett swooped down next to her on the divan and pulled her into his arms. "Shh, honey. Don't cry. It's all right. Whatever it is, it's all right."

Summer nestled against him, her head lodged beneath his chin, and basked in the warmth of his embrace.

"Summer," he said then, his voice sounding unusually timid, "you're not...regretting your decision, are you?"

She looked up and met his intense gaze, not quite able to believe he'd just asked her that. He hadn't asked her ever before, and at the moment, it was a question way too big to answer. Things had happened so rapidly since the morning he'd announced to his family that they were getting married that she still hadn't found the time or courage to broach the subject with him as she should have. As she'd acknowledged to herself before, she was just letting it all happen.

"We both know I didn't really get to *make* the decision," she told him, finally reining in her tears. "You made it for me that morning when your mother and sisters showed up at your apartment."

A heavy look of guilt shrouded Brett's normally easygoing expression. "I know it was awful of me," he admitted, dropping his gaze, "but I couldn't figure out how to make you say yes. So when I got the opportunity to put you in a tight spot, I took it. I'm a heel. I'm sorry."

Summer sighed. She'd known the truth all along, yet had somehow blocked it out or looked past it ever since the moment just afterward when she'd conceded and let him take her into his arms. Hearing him actually admit it, though, hit her full in the face. He'd tricked her. Coerced her. In short, he'd behaved like a jerk.

But he was sorry, and while Summer didn't really know what the future held, and still wondered how she'd gotten caught on this runaway train of a wedding, she somehow couldn't be mad.

"You're right," she said. "You were a huge heel."

"Can you forgive me?" he whispered, worry clouding his normally clear blue eyes.

A few weeks ago, Summer thought, she'd have told him there was no way in hell she could forgive him. A few weeks ago, she'd have taken any way out of this she could find. Yet things had changed since then, in a big way. "Yes," she said softly. "I can forgive you."

"Summer," he breathed, "I want so much to marry you. I'm so happy. I love you. I just...hope you're not crying because I've made you so miserable, or because you really don't want to marry me."

She shook her head and said, "It's not that."

"What then?"

Oh, how could she possibly explain it all? All the emotions, all the strange and unexpected joy. "It's just that...your mom...is so nice."

He smiled, obviously confused. "Yeah, she is."

"I'm just crying," she explained, "because she makes me feel like a real part of the family."

"You *are* a real part of the family," he said, lifting a hand lovingly to her cheek.

Infused with warmth, she covered his hand with her own.

"HEY, SUMMER, wait up!"

At the sound of her name, Summer stopped and looked over her shoulder in Stafford's parking garage to find Tina, each click of her heels echoing across the concrete floor. Summer sighed. She was late meeting Brett for dinner and really didn't have time to chat. He'd invited her to an exclusive restaurant in Mt. Adams for what he'd called "a special surprise."

"What's up?" she asked as Tina approached.

"Right as you were walking out, your phone rang, so I grabbed it," Tina said, breathless, then she smiled. "It was the bridal shop lady calling to say the veil you ordered is finished, and our bridesmaid dresses are in, too!"

"Wow, that's great," Summer said, but even to herself

she sounded distracted. "Thanks for letting me know, Tina—" she winced, feeling badly at having to cut the conversation short "—but I'm kind of in a rush."

"Oh." Tina gave her head a speculative tilt. "I guess I just thought you'd be excited about this stuff."

"I *am* excited," Summer replied, "but I'm running late. And thanks for catching up to let me know—you're the best maid of honor ever."

Still, Tina looked disappointed.

"What's wrong?" Summer asked, shifting from one foot to the other.

"Nothing," Tina replied, shaking her head, but looking uncharacteristically nervous.

"Something," Summer insisted. "Out with it."

Tina sighed. "It's just... I wasn't going to mention this, and maybe I shouldn't, because I guess you seem perfectly happy, but on the other hand, if I were getting married, I think I'd be more excited about every little detail of the wedding and—"

"Tina," Summer said, "what is it already?" She tried to smile as if this was nothing, but her chest had gone hollow.

"Summer, you know that besides being my boss, you're my best friend, right?"

They'd never actually called each other "best friend" before, but Summer certainly felt that way, too. She nodded.

"The thing is, I guess I just wanted to make sure that...well, that you know what you're doing. I know I haven't said anything through all the wedding planning, but I'm just a little worried that...maybe you're getting married for the wrong reasons."

Wow. Summer stood dumbfounded, her insides tied instantly in knots. Tina's words had totally knocked her for a loop. Maybe because she'd felt them, or feared them, too?

She was so happy to be joining Brett's family, and despite herself, even pleased at the prospect of creating a normal, loving, two-parent home for the child inside her. She knew she was lucky to have found a man as kind and sweet and dependable as Brett. Yet questions lingered. Her regular sense of control had abandoned her completely and she still wasn't sure of things. Was marrying him the right thing to do?

She took a deep breath and spoke very calmly. "What are the reasons why you think we're getting married?"

"I guess maybe I think you're getting married just because of the baby." Tina cringed, as if saying the words were painful.

And they were almost painful for Summer, too, but not quite, since they were so true. Or maybe it was simply the word *just* that felt offensive. Sure, she and Brett both knew they were getting married because of the baby, but was that really the *only* reason?

"It's not *just* because of the baby," she claimed.

"Then why else?"

Summer didn't answer. She knew there was more, much more, but the reasons wouldn't come to her in any simple, sensible way she could explain.

"I mean, I guess I'm just worried about you marrying a guy you don't love," Tina said, "even as great a guy as Brett is."

Summer's heart nearly burst with the strange anger that struck her then. Tina thought Summer didn't love him? She couldn't believe that her one, true friend in the world had just said such a thing! "For your information," Summer announced, "I *do* love Brett! Very much! I love him more than I can say!"

She managed to hold in the gasp that followed her own words, but the realization hit her like a bolt of lightning.

She *did* love him! And she couldn't wait to be his wife!

Oh my God! *"It's true,"* she exclaimed, almost as much to herself as to Tina. "I love him! I love him, I love him, I love him!"

Unforeseen joy rushed through Summer's veins. Relief! Elation! Happily ever after! She had it all! This would all be okay because *she loved Brett!*

No wonder she'd let the wedding train take her, and no wonder she'd been unable to stay mad at Brett for coercing her acceptance. She'd loved him all along and she wanted this, really wanted it—more than she'd wanted anything in a very long time! It had only taken this conversation, someone questioning her feelings, to make her finally understand it!

She saw Tina grinning at her then and realized she was clutching both of her friend's hands. "What?" Summer asked, shaking her head in confusion.

"I knew it all along," Tina said.

Summer's jaw dropped. "You did? But then why did you..."

"I guess I just wanted to make sure you knew it, too, and now you do. I've seen doubt in your eyes, seen you look so lost and worried at moments, and *I* think you're doing the right thing, but it's your *heart* that counts. So maybe...all that doubt will be gone now?"

Summer smiled at her friend. "Yeah. I think it's suddenly long gone." She bit her lip, still reeling from the revelation. "And you know, I really *am* excited about the dresses and the veil, but I'm just running late to meet Brett. We're having a special dinner tonight."

Tina raised her eyebrows suggestively. "Special? What's *that* mean?"

"I don't know exactly. Which is why I should..." She pointed vaguely in the direction of her car.

Tina gave her a small, friendly nudge. "Go," she said. "Go be with your man. I'm sorry I held you up."

"I'm not," Summer said, hoping the depth of her appreciation shone in her eyes when she added, "Thanks, Tina."

"Have a nice dinner," Tina said. "Ta ta." Then her footsteps went clicking away as quickly as they'd approached, leaving Summer to stand there, as dumbfounded as she'd been before, but for a much happier reason this time. She loved Brett with all her heart, and she couldn't wait to tell him!

BRETT CHECKED HIS WATCH, then glanced toward the doorway. Still no Summer.

He knew she liked to work late, and hoped that would change soon. He'd hoped it would change *tonight*, for starters, since he'd made dinner reservations, but apparently not.

"Still the lady does not arrive, sir?" a waiter with a thick, unrecognizable accent stopped to ask...again.

Brett attempted a smile as he shook his head, but he was beginning to feel embarrassed, because maybe the waiter—and everyone else in the restaurant, for that matter—thought perhaps there *was* no lady, that he was being stood up, or that maybe he was just some poor nut who'd imagined her.

He checked the time again, then watched as the waiter returned to pour more coffee into his cup. If Brett kept drinking it, he'd be completely wired by the time she showed up and he wouldn't be able to do what he'd wanted to do in just the right way. His proposals to her, many as there had been, had lacked something, something big. He'd tried to do it all properly from the very beginning, but circumstances hadn't permitted it. And after the talk they'd had at his mother's house the other day, following Summer's bridal shower, he'd realized he owed it to her to make this the most special time in her life. So that's exactly what he intended to do—give her one very special night she'd always remember—*if* she ever showed up.

He reached for the coffee, more out of boredom than thirst.

"Brett!"

He flinched at the sound and hot coffee spattered the back of his hand.

"Oh God, I'm so sorry!" It was Summer, looking frantic as she grabbed a mauve linen napkin from the table, practically diving to pat the coffee from his skin.

"It's all right, it's all right," he told her.

"No, it's not," she said, her green eyes wider than he'd ever seen them. "The last thing I want to do right now is make you spill coffee on yourself or do anything else to ruin this moment!"

"What moment?"

"The moment when I tell you that I love you!"

She stood over him, peering down, looking wildly beautiful and excited, and Brett could barely fathom the words she'd just said. He sat there trying to absorb them, but it didn't work—it didn't seem possible or real. "You love me?" he finally breathed.

She nodded enthusiastically.

He said it louder this time. "You really love me? Really? Like, you're..."

"In love with you," she said, loudly enough to attract attention from the next table. "Completely and totally!"

Okay, now it seemed real. Incredibly so.

The words propelled Brett out of his seat, and he took Summer into his arms, at the same time toppling the small table where he'd been sitting. "Oh damn," he muttered as cups and water glasses and silverware crashed to the floor around him. Yet Summer didn't seem to even notice, because she was too busy pulling him into a passionate kiss, and what could he do at a perfect moment in time like this but kiss her back?

"I see the lady has finally arrived."

Brett glanced up to find the waiter looking not even slightly amused. He shifted his gaze back to Summer and spoke quietly. "I have a feeling we're about to get kicked out of here."

"Who cares?" she replied merrily.

"Well," Brett said, feeling more than a little sheepish, since all eyes in the room were planted squarely on them now, "I wanted to be someplace nice to give you *this*." He pulled back from her, just enough to reach into his jacket and extract a black velvet box.

He loved Summer's delighted gasp and the way she splayed her fingers across her lips as he opened it to show her the diamond ring inside. "I hope you like it," he said. "If you don't, we can go shopping for another one together."

Summer shook her head emphatically. "No, I love it! It's beautiful! I wouldn't trade it for a million dollars! Put it on me, please."

Brett wanted nothing more than to do just that. He was still reeling from the knowledge that Summer was really and truly happy to be marrying him—that she actually *loved* him!—but the waiter continued scowling at them and it seemed none of the restaurant patrons were as caught up in their happiness as he might have expected. "Maybe we should...go someplace else. I mean, I want this to be special. Perfect."

Yet Summer simply smiled up at him, a radiant light shining in her eyes. "Remember when we met at Dunbar's? That was perfect. And remember when you brought picnic lunches to work and we ate on the floor of my office? That was perfect, too. I once thought perfection had to do with things like champagne and caviar, but...oh, never mind all that. The point is, every place is perfect with you, Brett."

She punctuated the statement by wrapping her arms around his neck and lifting another long, deep kiss to his mouth, making him forget where he was for a minute, and forget to care, as well. Only when a few romantic oohs and ahhs finally came wafting from the dining crowd did he remember and reluctantly break the kiss. The annoyed waiter said, "Would you put the ring on her finger already?"

Brett gazed tenderly down into the eyes of the woman he loved, then lifted the marquise-shaped diamond ring from the velvet box and carefully slid it onto the third finger of Summer's left hand while the crowd watched. They applauded when he was done, completely won over now despite the interruption to their dinner, but Brett couldn't hear anything, couldn't see anything, except for the twinkle of love in Summer's beautiful green eyes.

6

THE WEDDING PLANS WERE complete now and most of the prewedding parties over. There was suddenly time to breathe, and adjust, and learn to love each other. And that's just what Summer and Brett began to do in the early days of June that followed—spend most of their time in bed, loving.

Summer was still trying to get used to the idea of being *in love* with him. It still seemed too good to be true! The future lay like a huge rolling landscape that had been unfurled just for them. They would embark on their own private journey, the journey of sharing life with a partner.

Summer lay in bed one morning, eyes still shut, thinking how it had all happened so fast. How could she be so happy, so suddenly? But none of the questions mattered anymore. She *was* happy and that was all that counted.

When a tiny kiss came high on her breast, the inner flutter it created rippled all the way to her toes. She opened her eyes and smiled at the man she would soon marry.

"Morning, beautiful." He gazed at her as if she were the most incredible thing he'd ever seen.

She treated him to a soft, coquettish look. "Morning."

"Thank you," he whispered throatily near her ear.

She raised her eyebrows as if to ask, *For what?*

"For last night. I think we must have set a record of some kind."

She bit her lip, remembering. She'd lost count of how many times they'd made love, how many times he'd told her he loved her, how many times she'd said the same words to him.

"It was my pleasure," she said.

"Well, if there's one thing I like," he replied, brushing his fingertips playfully over the cleft between her legs, "it's bringing you pleasure."

She giggled, then nuzzled against him, resting her cheek against his strong shoulder.

"What I want to know now," he said, "is what changed?"

"Hmm?" she asked, deliciously lost in the wonder of love.

"What changed?" he asked again. "Until a few days ago, I still felt like I was twisting your arm into marrying me. Now I don't. Now you say you love me like it's the easiest thing in the world." He pulled back just enough to meet her gaze. "Don't get me wrong, honey, I'm not complaining. I just wonder what caused this sudden transformation in my beautiful wife-to-be."

In all honesty, Summer was surprised he hadn't asked her about this before now. She supposed they'd just been too caught up in each other to pause for much serious discussion.

Since he'd asked, though, she didn't mind telling him the truth. That's what good marriages were built on, right? And the new, *in love* Summer had vowed to herself that that's what they would have—a good marriage.

"It just hit me out of nowhere," she began, rising up on her elbow to gaze down at him. "I was actually talking to Tina about it, about why I was getting married, and suddenly I realized that I loved you. I know now that if I didn't love you, I would never have let myself be talked into it. I think I wanted this all along, Brett, but I was just fighting it."

"Wow," he said, looking a little taken aback. "That makes me...really happy."

She gave him a smile. "I'm glad, because that's what I want. To make you happy."

His eyes shone then like crystal marbles. He looked completely in awe at her words, completely in awe of *her*.

"Although you should quit lying there looking so thoroughly taken with me, because..." She trailed off, uncertainty sneaking in, until she reminded herself that she was going to be entirely honest. "Because I still have some niggling doubts about...well, giving up my independence. Control of my life, and control of the baby's life. I've been the sole decision-maker for myself for so long that it's an almost innate part of me, and I'm still not sure how I'm going to cope with giving that up."

"But you must think you can," he pointed out, "or you wouldn't suddenly be so happy about marrying me."

She sighed and cast him a sheepish look. "I kind of just pushed those worries aside," she admitted.

"See there," he said, surprising her with his notorious crooked grin, "that's a good start. Because sometimes that's just what you have to do."

She flinched slightly, not sure she agreed. "It is? Just push things aside? Is that healthy?"

"The way I see it," Brett said, "marriage is give and take, and sometimes that means compromise. And sometimes compromise means pushing your wants aside."

Summer frowned. "I've never liked compromise."

"Trust me," he said, laughing, "I'll make it worth your while." Then he rolled over in bed until he lay on top of her, and he kissed her, slow and deep, his tongue easing past her lips, his hands dropping beneath the covers.

SUMMER STOOD SIDEWAYS before the mirror in her bedroom—soon to be her and *Brett's* bedroom—and studied her newly expanding stomach through the roomy cotton pajamas she'd just put on, smoothing her hand down over her belly. At four months, she was legitimately showing now. She would need to shop for maternity clothes very soon.

Why did she have to be showing so early? But then, she remembered knowing plenty of other women who'd been showing by this point, too, and she also recalled her doctor's prediction. *That's what I get for being petite.*

Not that it really mattered. She was pregnant and was supposed to look this way. Still, she thought she looked much bigger than she had only a few days before, and she couldn't help thinking that this wasn't at all what she'd planned for her summer. She'd thought she might rent a condo in Florida for a week or two and lounge around in a bikini soaking up the rays. Now she looked like she'd soaked up a lot more than just rays, and as for a bikini? Not a chance!

Of course, when she rationalized, she realized that nothing was really wrong here. She was still madly in love with her husband-to-be, and happier than she'd ever imagined such changes could make her. So maybe this was just hormonal or something. She just felt fat, and a little bit scared. She was going a have a baby soon, for heaven's sake! Why couldn't she have met Brett and had some kind of normal relationship with him before this happened?

"Hey gorgeous, why the frown?"

She looked up to see Brett standing behind her wearing a T-shirt and jeans, the same jeans with the rip in the knee she remembered from the fateful night of their second lovemaking. He'd been downstairs adding some of his books to her shelves in the living room.

She gave her head a forlorn shake. "I guess I...just wish you could have seen me before I was fat."

"I *did* see you before you were fat, remember?"

Summer gasped. "You think I'm fat?"

He tilted his head and sighed. "Honey, you're not fat. You're beautiful like this." As if to prove his words, he circled his arms around her from behind and began to caress her rounded belly through the cotton that shrouded it.

"But I feel...so unattractive."

"Shh," he whispered, his breath tickling her ear. "Close your eyes."

Summer drew in her breath and did as Brett asked. The length of his body pressed warmly against hers as he continued to move his hands over her belly and then her breasts, and soon she felt him beginning to grow hard against her bottom.

She opened her eyes to see his fingers working at the buttons on her pajama top. Then he stepped back to slide the top from her shoulders, on which he bestowed a slow barrage of sweet, tiny kisses.

"You really want me like this?" she couldn't help asking as she studied herself, bared to the waist. She knew she wasn't *that* big yet, but she was certainly bigger than she'd ever been before.

"I really do," he whispered. "Now let's go to bed."

Brett lay Summer tenderly across the comforter on the bed he now shared with her most nights. What she didn't know, he thought, was that she wasn't the only person who had some anxiety over how rapidly both their lives were changing. It was hard for him to believe he would soon leave his beloved apartment to come share this house with her. And even as much as he was looking forward to it, it was difficult to fathom that soon he would become a father.

Yet he loved Summer madly and he knew love would see them through this. Now that he knew she loved him, too...well, he'd do whatever it took to make her happy. And making love to her would make them *both* happy. He wanted to be inside her, wanted to feel their bodies joined just as he had that first night when all this had begun.

He pulled off her pajama bottoms and underwear, then stripped off his own clothes, too. Kneeling over her in the bed, he lowered soft kisses to her breasts, swelling now from the pregnancy, and then he kissed her belly. He thought it was as if he were kissing the baby inside, as well. "Hi, little guy," he whispered next to her.

Above him, she giggled. "You're still sure this is going to be a boy, huh?"

He nodded. "Absolutely."

Soon Brett rolled Summer onto her side and lay behind her. Whispering "I love you" close to her ear, he eased his way into her waiting body. "How does that feel?"

"Good," she responded breathily.

"I read that this is the best position during the later months," he said.

She glanced over her shoulder at him, clearly surprised. "Been reading up on pregnancy, have you?"

He nodded, quietly proud.

"Although it's only June," she pointed out teasingly. "I don't think this qualifies as the later months."

"Practice," he whispered, and then he began to move gently inside her. "Still good?"

"Mmm," she replied. He liked it when she answered him like that—it always told him he was doing things right.

As his urgency increased, Brett reached over her hip and dipped his fingers between her thighs. "Oh..." she breathed, and he knew he wasn't the only one feeling urgent anymore. They moved together, him against her, her against his hand, until sweet ecstasy took them both, almost at the same time.

Brett held her tightly afterward, listening to the sounds of both of them breathing, just thinking how perfect, how wonderful it all was. It didn't matter what obstacles lay before them—moments like this made it all go away.

"You're so beautiful," he whispered a minute later when she lay snuggled against him, her face nestled against his chest. He almost felt her smile, and he sensed her sleepiness in the heavy way she lay on him. "Tired?" he asked.

"Mmm-hmm."

"You need to start taking it easy, honey," he said gently.

"Hmm?" She lifted her head slightly.

"I said you need to start slowing down some. I read that as the pregnancy progresses, you need to start heeding your body's signals, and that if your body is telling you you're tired, you need to take it easy."

Suddenly, she was wide-awake and peering up at him, looking completely disgruntled. "Well, my doctor says I can do the same things I normally do as long as I feel like doing them."

"Isn't that what I just said?"

"No, it's not."

"I mean, if your body doesn't feel like being as active," he tried to explain again, "you should rest. After all, you work until seven or eight every night and that can't be good. Can't you start leaving at five like normal people?" he suggested tentatively.

"No, I can't. My job is everything, Brett. You know that."

"But soon it won't be."

"What do you mean?"

He lifted a hand to her cheek, then told her what he thought was obvious. "Soon the baby will be more important than anything, Summer."

She simply looked at him and he got the idea that she understood the weight of his words, that she knew they were true, but that perhaps this had never occurred to her before.

"This is where compromise starts coming into play," he told her gingerly. He didn't want to make her any madder than she already appeared to be, but they'd both known she would have to start facing this.

"And I told you," she said, sounding sad as she lowered her head next to his, "I'm not very good with compromise."

"Well—" he turned on his side to face her "—I have a feeling you're gonna have to start trying to be. And not just because of me, either," he pointed out, "but for the baby." An urge for silence and gentleness swept over him like a calming breeze then, and he kissed her forehead and whispered for her to go to sleep.

"But, Brett," she protested, sounding exhausted.

"Shh, sleep now. We can talk more later," he said, sorry he'd broached such a large issue so unthinkingly.

He'd forgotten, he supposed, just how huge she considered the sacrifices she'd have to make. Sacrifices for the baby, and actually, for him, too. She'd been right—getting married meant she would have a say in his decisions, and that he would have a say in hers. Right now, he couldn't help expressing his feelings about her pregnancy and expecting her to take them seriously.

But it had been thoughtless of him to just throw it at her when they were both tired after lovemaking, and it wasn't so urgent that they couldn't sleep on it. She had to face this, he thought, but not all at once. She'd promised to marry him, and that in itself had been a huge compromise. As for the rest of it, it could wait at least until tomorrow.

SUMMER SPENT the next days walking around work experiencing alternate bouts of depression and anger. This compromise stuff was going to be just as hard as she'd imagined. The depression part was because she *was* tired, she *did* need to slow down, and she would have to find ways to delegate more responsibilities to others whether she liked it or not. The anger part was more like annoyance, and it was because he'd been right, and because, suddenly, just as she'd feared, she felt she had no control over her life at all. She'd decided to marry Brett and already he'd started making decisions for her.

Still, she loved him and knew he would be a wonderful father, and she also knew his heart was in the right place with the baby's concerns. So she would have to try.

"Tina," she called when she spotted her friend approaching down the hallway that led to the accounting department. They met halfway and Summer took a deep breath, trying to force herself through step one of this torture called compromise. "Listen, tell me if you think you can't handle it, but I was wondering how you'd feel about taking on the monthly volume report and maybe the quarterly departmental budget calculations."

Summer held her breath, almost hoping that Tina would say no, that it would be too much heaped upon her current workload.

"Actually," Tina replied with a smile, "I would *love* to have more responsibility. And working on the budget calcs will allow me more interaction with the departmental managers, won't it?"

Summer stood strong. "You're right, it will."

"Then it sounds great to me," Tina said, placing a friendly hand on Summer's wrist. "And, Summer, don't hesitate to ask if there's anything else I can do. Especially while you're away on your honeymoon, or later, when you're on maternity leave."

Summer simply nodded. She couldn't ask for a better employee, or a better friend. "Thanks," she said, even though, despite her appreciation, her happiness was only halfhearted. "Well, I've gotta run. Late for a meeting with Metzger in shipping."

She dashed down the hall, feeling almost woozy that she'd just handed such a huge task off to Tina, not to mention that the entire buying department would be in Tina's hands for at least three months after the baby was born.

Yet, Summer reminded herself, things had to be this way. Brett was right—the baby would have to come first. She could do this. She could. *Just stay in control,* she told herself, beginning to relax a little.

Funny, she thought. It was a whole different kind of control she sought now. She was no longer attempting to keep total control over herself and her life, but instead trying to find the control—the will—to let go of all that.

That night she tried to leave by five, but didn't make it. Still, she thought as she pushed the button for the elevator and then glanced at her watch, five-thirty was much better than usual.

When she got home twenty minutes later, Brett's car sat in the driveway. He hadn't officially moved in yet, but he may as well have. A steady stream of his belongings continued to make their way into her house, and he'd spent most nights there lately, as well. She couldn't deny liking his nearness, the comfort of coming home to him. If this was a taste of marriage, then she was going to like it.

Inside, the downstairs was quiet—no Brett—but then Summer made her way up the steps, suddenly lured by the pungent scent of wet paint. She followed the smell to the room she'd told him she wanted to make into a nursery, and was stopped in the doorway by the sight before her.

Brett wore a T-shirt and gym shorts, an old baseball cap turned backward on his head...all spattered with dots of pastel paint. Concentrating on his work, he didn't even see her come in. The room, which just this morning had been white, now bore one wall of pale yellow, one of mint green, one of light blue, and the fourth was in the process of becoming lavender. A border displaying brightly colored balloons, teddy bears and kites lay curled at his feet.

"That's kind of a soft color for a boy, don't you think?" she asked teasingly, nodding toward the lavender wall.

He looked up with a start, an expression of worry instantly clouding his gaze. "Don't kill me," he said. "I know I should've asked your opinion, but I wanted to surprise you. And—" he suddenly looked puzzled "—what the hell are you doing here so early, anyway?"

"I took your advice," she told him, "and left work on time. Well, at least, more on time than usual."

He flashed the smile she loved, and said, "That's great," his voice warm and sweet, then turning playful. "But I could've used a little warning. I meant to have this done before you got home."

"Why don't I change into something old and we can work on it together?" she suggested.

"Sounds good," he said with a grin. "I asked at the hardware store to make sure I got the right kind of paint so there wouldn't be any harmful fumes."

She smiled at his attention to her and the baby, something that never seemed to waver, before taking another glance around the room. "This all looks so wonderful."

He tilted his head. "So you don't mind that I picked out this stuff without you? Because if you do, we can start over. We can take it all back—"

"No, I love it," she said, cutting him off. "Nice border, too," she added, pointing to where it lay across the floor.

He picked up the roll and held it out, so she could see it better. The balloons and kites and bears all contained bolder shades of the colors on the walls—a royal blue, a kelly green, a sunshiny yellow and a vivid purple. "Babies like bright colors," he said.

"I know," she replied, thinking he was incredibly cute. "We must be reading the same books."

A few minutes later, Summer had changed into an old pair of drawstring pants and a big T-shirt, and joined Brett in the nursery. He finished painting the last wall and suggested she start painting the baseboards white.

"I stuck the white paint in the closet over there," he said, pointing with his paint roller.

Summer padded to the designated closet, one of two in the room. Located against the outside of the house, it contained one of the deep slopes she'd told Brett about when they'd first started getting acquainted.

When she opened the door, a burst of fresh color greeted her. To her immense surprise, Brett had painted the inside of the closet a light shade of peach. The sight made her gasp in delight.

Her heart flushed with a whole new sense of love for him as she leaned around the closet door to give him a curious smile. He must have caught sight of it from the corner of his eye, since he stopped rolling the lavender paint over the wall long enough to return her look. "What?"

"You painted the inside of the closet," she said, still smiling.

Did he look a little sheepish about her discovery? "Yeah, well, the inside of the other one is pink now. Last pastel I could come up with, so I hid it in the closet to keep the little guy tough," he added with an easy laugh.

Summer joined in his laughter, still warmed by the trouble he'd gone to, then turned back to get the white paint.

"You know," he said, "I was thinking." She looked up to find him pointing again toward the sloped closet with his paint roller. "If we took that door off, it would be a good place to store bigger toys, and it might make a nice play area when he's a little older, kind of like a private playhouse or a fort or something. What do you think? Bad idea?"

Summer tilted her head. God, she loved this man, and

she loved his thoughtfulness regarding their child. "No, I think it's a wonderful idea."

"Really? Because I don't want to start making all the decisions on my own here, or suggesting we change the whole house around or anything."

Summer shook her head. "No, that's not what you're doing at all."

He cast her a soft smile. "As long as you're sure."

"Don't worry," she said. "I am."

Summer finally got the white paint from the newly tinted peach closet and went to work on the baseboards. Soon Brett had finished the lavender wall, and he joined her painting the trim. As they worked, he told her that Jackie had offered to give them the baby bed she'd used for both her kids. He assured Summer that it was like new, and that it was white, which would match the trimwork. "I was thinking of building some shelves, too," he added. "Painting them white and hanging them next to the closet. For books or whatever. That sound good to you?"

Summer's heart warmed once more, nearly to bursting this time. It would be impossible not to love this guy! "I think that would be perfect."

She also thought that life itself was beginning to seem perfect, and that maybe giving up control wasn't quite as bad as she'd thought. After all, she hadn't worried about work since she'd left, or even about the responsibilities she'd handed over to Tina today. And something that normally might have made her feel intruded upon—Brett picking the nursery decor—had instead touched and even thrilled her.

She'd given up control, yet look at all she'd gained— laughter, comfort, security, support and a surprising new hope for the future.

She'd gained something else, too, something she'd never expected to have, or never even thought she'd wanted. But she'd been wrong about that part. She *did* want it, and deep down inside she'd probably wanted it all along. It was the source of all the new hope in her heart.

She'd gained a loving husband and a child.

She'd gained a family of her own.

IN THE DAYS THAT FOLLOWED, Summer worked hard not to work too hard. She delegated a few more responsibilities, started training Tina on what to do when she went on leave, and most days managed to get away at five or a few minutes after.

There were moments when it became difficult, when that controlling part of her urged her to stay and complete a project, or when it felt strange to have to share common everyday decisions with someone else. Regardless, Summer worked her way through those times and by the end of the week felt stronger and more secure for the effort.

When she arrived home on Friday night, she found Brett standing over the stove, stirring meat sauce and boiling spaghetti in a large pan one of his aunts had given them as a shower gift. "Hey, what's the special occasion?" she asked, slipping out of her shoes.

He tossed her a half smile. "No special occasion. Except that it's Friday and I thought I'd cook dinner for my soon-to-be wife." His grin grew. "Wife," he repeated. "I like saying that."

Summer's heart swelled when she stepped into the dining room to see two long taper candles twinkling, a solitary rose peeking from a bud vase in between. She splayed a hand across her chest. "This is lovely, Brett."

"Yeah, well," he said with a tilt of his head, "consider it a sample of all the good husband stuff to come."

They shared a quiet dinner, discussing Summer's day at work, and then Brett's. With a smile, he informed her of the purchase he'd made after work—a set of jumper cables. "I'll put them in your trunk later," he told her.

"Why?"

"In case you're ever stranded again. Besides, I was just thinking, it seems okay for a single guy not to have jumper cables, but a husband, and a dad, should be responsible enough to have them."

Seeing how proud he was of the idea, Summer said, "Well, I'll feel much more secure now when I'm out driving around."

"Although I have to admit," he added, "I'm glad neither one of us had them the night we met."

Summer playfully raised her eyebrows at him over the shimmering candles. "Oh? And why is that?"

He grinned his crooked grin. "You'd have gotten away."

After that, Brett did what he'd been doing *every* day lately: he asked Summer how she was feeling. She didn't mind, though, and in fact, she'd grown to cherish how much he cared.

"Now," he said when dinner was over, "on to surprise number two."

Summer let her eyes widen. "There's more?"

He nodded, looking mischievous, then pulled out her chair, took her hand and led her to the bedroom. In the middle of the bed lay a white box topped with a lavender bow. "A present?" she said. "Brett, you didn't have to buy me a present."

"I know I didn't have to," he said. "I wanted to."

"But—"

"No buts," he stated, cutting her off. "You'll understand when you see it."

Summer sat on the bed, and Brett sat next to her. She took the lid off the box and found a filmy piece of lavender fabric that, as she pulled it from the box, she couldn't quite make sense of. Brett had been wrong saying she'd understand when she saw it, because she didn't.

Seeing her puzzlement, he reached to turn the fabric in her hands. "It goes this way."

The fabric began to take on a sort of shape then. She saw what she thought were places meant for breasts, and openings for arms, but she still didn't quite get it. "What exactly...is it?" she asked, feeling a smidge embarrassed.

"It's a maternity negligee," he said, his voice brimming with pride.

She could suddenly see it then. She'd been right about the places where the breasts were supposed to go, and the remaining transparent fabric was made to fall like a veil over her tummy.

"See," he said, "it opens up here in the front, so no matter how big you get, you'll always fit. You hardly need any of this room yet, but I figure this'll last us right up until B-day."

"B-day?"

He grinned. "Baby day."

Summer thought this was incredibly sweet of him, and terribly romantic, but... "Brett, you know I'm not crazy about showing off my body right now."

"That's why I got it," he said. "Because you *should* be crazy about showing off your body. At least to me, I mean," he said with a short laugh.

"But... Brett, I don't know...." It was really a lovely

nightie, but she couldn't quite imagine herself trying to be sexy in it, especially in the months to come.

"Please, Summer," he said, seeming to read her mind. "Put it on. For me. Then if you still feel the same about it, you can take it off. Besides," he added, "I went to a lot of trouble to find it."

She looked up at him. "And just how *did* you find such a garment?"

"I went from sexy nightie department to sexy nightie department in every store in the mall, asking every saleswoman I saw."

Summer couldn't help smiling at the picture it created in her mind. He *had* gone to a lot of trouble. "Where'd you finally get it?"

"Downtown at Stafford's, of course."

Summer laughed. She'd had no idea her own store stocked maternity lingerie, but she was sort of glad. She wasn't sure whether she actually liked it or not for herself, but felt proud at knowing they were on the cutting edge.

"So," he said, looking persuasive, "will you at least try it on and see what you think?"

Summer released a long sigh, offering a half smile and a conceding nod. She really couldn't believe some of the things Brett had the ability to talk her into, and when she weighed her options, she supposed that compared to getting married, this was nothing. "All right," she agreed. "But go...amuse yourself elsewhere for a few minutes or something."

He smiled devilishly. "Building suspense," he said. "I like that." Then he disappeared out the door and left Summer alone with her new lavender maternity negligee.

She felt a little ridiculous taking all her clothes off and

pulling the filmy fabric over her head in her slightly expanded condition. Again she had the yearning to do things like this with Brett *without* being pregnant. How fun it would have been to slip on something sleek and sexy for him back when she had a nice shape, but this...this felt a little silly.

She tugged the nightie into place, arranging the loose fabric so it flowed over her growing tummy, then turned to the mirror.

Studying herself, she didn't quite know what she felt at first. The fabric was completely see-through, so there was nothing left to the imagination—this was simply decorating the package, so to speak. But it *was* feminine. And romantic. And dare she think *sexy?*

"Ready yet?" Brett's voice came from just beyond the doorway.

"Um, yeah," she replied, still feeling a little sheepish.

The moment he stepped through the door, however, all that changed. He'd stripped to his briefs, and Summer could instantly see the evidence of his arousal. And when their gazes met in the mirror, and she watched his eyes take in her body, she began to feel...beautiful.

"Look at you," he breathed, stepping up behind her, placing his hands softly on her shoulders. "Look at how incredible you are. Look at how perfect."

"You really think so?" She hated to ask the question, but she needed to hear more of his whispered assurances.

"Yes, honey. I think you're...beyond beautiful."

"You say that now," she said, peeking playfully over her shoulder. "But how will you feel at eight or nine months?"

He grinned. "I'll still think you're just as beautiful. Promise."

"One thing, Brett," she said cautiously, biting her lip. "I didn't find any panties or bottoms of any kind in the box."

A wicked grin took shape on his face. "I didn't think we'd need 'em."

With that, he gently pulled her onto the bed, kissing and caressing her, ready to show her just how beautiful she was. He'd questioned whether it was wise to push such a gift on her while he knew she was starting to feel unattractive, but now he was glad he had. He hoped she could see just how lovely she was to him, hoped he'd helped her understand the beauty he saw in her, pregnant or not.

"Why'd you do all this?" she asked, nibbling his ear in a way that vibrated all through him.

"Well," he said, "remember when we talked about give and take?"

She nodded.

"I know you've been giving in on some things lately," he explained, "and I've been doing my fair share of taking—asking you to come home earlier and not work so hard. I don't feel like I've been giving much, though, so I thought this might be a good way to start."

He pushed his arousal suggestively against her hip and she released a low groan, just the kind he loved. "I think you give plenty," she told him.

"Does that mean you don't want it?" he asked playfully, starting to pull away from her.

She grabbed his neck and yanked him back against her. "Don't even think about it, mister."

A FEW DAYS LATER, Summer lay stretched across a doctor's table in a small room filled with complicated-looking machinery, her bared abdomen freezing cold and slimy from the jellylike substance smeared across it. Her obstetrician stood next to her, firmly pressing a metal contraption across her tummy. Summer was dying to go to the bathroom and all she could think of was getting this over with. She found it hard to enjoy lying in this most inelegant position while her husband-to-be smiled over her.

Just then she heard Brett pull in his breath, and she followed his eyes to a small black-and-white monitor. "Look, Summer," he breathed.

She was looking. It was...the baby. *Their* baby. Her stomach pinched and her throat tightened with unexpected emotion. Without planning it, she reached out and grabbed Brett's hand.

He gently squeezed her fingers as Dr. Norris began pointing to the screen, outlining the baby's head, arms, tiny curled legs. Without the doctor's help, it would have been difficult to know what they were looking at, but once the body parts were identified, the whole picture became clearer. Summer swallowed and Brett tightened his grip on her hand even more. Daring to shift her gaze from the monitor to Brett, she saw that his eyes had turned glassy as he watched what they'd made together.

"I'll label the parts for you," the gray-haired doctor said, turning to a keyboard. A moment later words like *head*, *foot* and *arm* appeared on the screen in the appropriate places.

"I know you listened to the heartbeat on your last visit, Summer," Dr. Norris said, "but would you like to hear it, too, Brett?"

He looked like an awestruck little boy as he gave an enthusiastic nod, and the doctor drew out the special stethoscope-like object Summer recalled from before. A moment later, Brett had it to his ears and was shifting his gaze from the doctor to Summer. "Oh, wow! I can't believe it—our baby's heart beating! You've already heard this?" he asked Summer.

She smiled and nodded. "But when you're done, I wouldn't mind hearing it again."

The doctor moved the stethoscope's ear pieces from Brett's head to Summer's, and even though she'd already listened to the heartbeat several weeks earlier, the whooshing sound of it touched her heart all over again with how real and alive their child was.

"Look," the doctor said, smiling as he peered back to the screen, "the baby is sucking its thumb."

He pointed out the specifics on the monitor and, clearly mesmerized, Brett said, "He can do that already?"

The doctor nodded. "Pretty amazing, isn't it?"

Brett looked dumbfounded for a moment, then smiled down at Summer. "I think that's one talented little guy we've got in there."

"Speaking of the 'little guy,'" the doctor said, "were you interested in discussing the baby's sex?"

"No," Summer answered quickly. "We want to be surprised."

"*One* of us wants to be surprised," Brett added. "The other one of us already knows."

The doctor raised his eyebrows. "Well-studied in ultrasounds, are you?"

Brett grinned and shook his head, all signs of mistiness disappearing from his eyes. "Nope, Doc, just got a hunch."

"And that hunch is?"

Brett glanced teasingly at Summer, then back to Dr. Norris, dropping his voice to a loud whisper. "She refuses to believe it, but just between you and me, I know it's a boy."

WHEN BRENDA CALLED BRETT at work the next morning with an invitation to lunch, he was more than a little ambivalent about going. He couldn't help being worried that she'd start harping at him again, telling him he shouldn't give up Paris in order to marry Summer, and he didn't want to hear it. Especially not after yesterday. Seeing his child moving, living inside Summer, had shored up his feelings for them both in a way that even *he* hadn't expected. Nothing in his life had ever felt more right than this.

But to his surprise, when he arrived at Pigall's, the downtown eatery Brenda had suggested, his sister was all smiles. "Wedding plans all set?" she asked after Brett ordered his lunch.

He nodded. "With everybody pitching in, it all worked out much easier than I'd have thought."

"Good," Brenda said, reaching for a bread stick in the basket between them on the table. "And that's...kind of what I wanted to talk to you about."

Uh-oh, he knew it. *Here it comes.* "What is?"

"The wedding."

He tilted his head and flashed his sister a hard look of warning, yet it seemed to leave her completely undaunted.

"I wanted to tell you, Brett, that I'm sorry I doubted your decision, and that I'm very happy for you."

Brett's mouth dropped open. He couldn't believe it. But if Brenda was anything, she was generally truthful, and she *did* look completely sincere. "Really?"

She nodded. "Really."

"Because I love her, Bren, and I can't wait to marry her, and have a baby with her, and—"

"Stop," she said, laughing, holding up one hand. "I know you love her. That's become clear to me. And I'm sorry I wasn't more supportive in the beginning. It just came along so suddenly, and I wasn't sure you were doing the right thing, but now I realize you are and that everything happens for a reason, and this must've happened for a reason, too. So I want to apologize for not being a very good sister lately, and for not being very nice to Summer so far. But I promise, that's going to change."

Brenda's words warmed Brett's heart. "Thanks, Bren," he said. "It means a lot to know you're on my side."

"I've always been on your side."

"I know, but I mean—"

"My only regret in all this, Brett," she said, cutting him off, her voice wistful, "is that you still have to give up Paris."

Give up Paris. The words had begun to seem ridiculously meaningless to Brett over the months since he'd made his decision. In fact, he'd practically forgotten all about it what with the excitement of falling in love with Summer, planning their wedding, preparing for the baby.

He thought then about Summer having to give up her *own* dreams in order to be with her parents during their last days, and about how every decision you made mapped out your course, led you on a particular path. Summer was a good, happy, loving person. Clearly, sacrificing her dreams for something important had not ruined her life. In fact, it suddenly dawned on him that they'd likely never have met without those decisions she'd been forced to make over ten years earlier. So the sacrifice he'd made about Paris seemed truly small, and truly as if it were meant to be.

"It's not as big a sacrifice as you probably think," he finally told his sister in reply. "Because look at all I'm getting in return."

"HAVE YOU GUYS started picking names yet?" Susan asked across the table.

The entire family had gathered at Brett's parents' house for a Sunday afternoon dinner. It was late June, the wedding was only a month away and this was the first social occasion Summer had spent with them all that didn't involve wedding planning. She discovered that Brett's brothers-in-law were just as friendly as the rest of the group, and she found all their kids delightful, as well. She instantly liked knowing her child would be raised alongside them, in their company. As dinner progressed, Summer thought it even seemed that Brenda might be warming up to her.

"Well," Brett replied, plucking a roll from a large bowl in the center of the long table, "we haven't, but now is as good a time as any." He turned to Summer. "What would you think about Andrew? Or Alexander, Alex for short?"

"I like Alex," she said.

"Or what about...Ethan? Or Evan?"

"Ethan, yes," she replied with a smile. "Evan, no."

"Why not?"

"Evan sounds like a rich boy."

Brett laughed. "With any luck, maybe he *will* be."

"What about a good, strong family name?" Brett's dad asked, grinning. "Like...Stanley."

A small, collective moan blanketed the table, and Susan rolled her eyes.

"Okay, what about girl names?" Jackie asked.

Summer cast a skeptical glance at Brett, then said, "Your brother is under the distinct impression that this baby is going to be a boy."

"Have you had your ultrasound yet?" Susan asked.

Summer and Brett exchanged a warm look before he answered. "Yeah, but we asked the doctor not to tell us. Since I *know* it's going to be a boy," he added, his bravado returning.

"And just how do you *know* it's going to be a boy?" Brenda asked.

Brett took a long look around the room. Of his sisters' children, four of the five were girls. "Let's just say we're due."

Light laughter rippled around the table, most of it coming from Brett's three brothers-in-law. "You said it, buddy," Jackie's husband agreed, reaching across for a high five.

An hour later, the ladies had retired to the living room and the men had ventured outdoors to play with the kids. Summer let her gaze wander to the window to watch Brett showing his nephew how to wear a baseball mitt, and her heart somersaulted at the sight. She recalled Brett's fond memories of his own Little League days with his father, and she realized all over again how right he'd been to want their child to have them both in his or her life. It had all happened quickly, but that didn't hamper the strange contentment she felt. This was all working out, just as it should have.

"I know what you're thinking," Susan chimed, drawing Summer's attention back inside. "You're thinking about how adorable he's gonna be with *your* baby."

Summer smiled in reply. No truer words could have been spoken.

"It's fascinating, really," Jackie mused. "The changes they go through."

Everyone laughed and Susan added, "Yep, one day they're virile, manly, macho men, and the next day they're cooing and talking in baby voices, and it's the cutest thing you've ever seen."

"Brett's been wonderful since the very beginning," Summer found the courage to confide. "Since the moment he found out I was expecting, he's been ready to be a daddy."

The women shared a collective smile, even Brenda, who was still being much nicer to her than ever before. It put Summer's heart at ease to realize she'd apparently, finally, won Brenda over. She didn't know how it had happened, she was only glad that it had. This meant that *everything* had fallen into place now, with no exceptions.

"Who wants a piece of my fresh apple pie?" Lois asked, getting to her feet.

When each of the women answered in the affirmative, Summer offered to help, but Jackie insisted she'd assist her mother instead. "You stay here and enjoy watching the boys out the window," she said with a wink.

"In the meantime, I'm gonna go start rounding up my troops," Susan said of her husband and two-year-old daughter. "We'll need to leave as soon as I eat my pie. Our neighbors are having a block party and I promised we'd stop in before it was over."

Suddenly alone with Brenda, Summer made a quick decision to "seal" the new, pleasant feelings between them. She didn't necessarily want to bring up an ugly topic, but she felt the need to clear the air. "Brenda," she said daringly, "I hope you and I will be able to put any bad feelings behind us now."

She knew it was a rash move, yet being spontaneous had proven not to be so bad over recent months, at least where Brett was concerned. It had just struck her that she didn't want to live with even a hint of leftover animosity between her and Brenda if she could do anything to change it. Perhaps if she was bold enough to take this first step, Brenda would acknowledge whatever problem had stood between them and they could lay it to rest completely before the wedding.

"I've been meaning to apologize to you about that, Summer. I hope you understand that it was nothing personal—I was just looking out for my brother's well-being. I wasn't sure he was doing the right thing by marrying you, but you clearly make him very happy, so I want to tell you that I'm happy for you both." She smiled as she spoke, and this time, Summer noticed, the smile reached her eyes.

"He makes me very happy, too," Summer assured her. "And I'm glad to know we have your approval."

"I'm glad to give it, and I'm just sorry I was such a stick-in-the-mud up until now. After all, I'm sure it's obvious to you how important family is to Brett." She glanced toward the window.

Summer nodded, looking back outside, as well, to where Brett sat in the grass assisting one of his tiny nieces in mastering the Etch-A-Sketch. It was more than obvious, and she loved that about him.

"He's determined to do the best thing for you and the baby. He's told me so more than once."

Drawing her gaze back inside, Summer swallowed, trying to decipher Brenda's last words. They didn't hold even a hint of malice, yet she instantly felt the need to point out that she and the baby weren't charity cases. "Well, yes, I think Brett wants the best for his child, and for me, and for *himself*, too."

Brenda shrugged. "Of course. Brett is happy. I should quit worrying about it. I'm probably the only one who's still concerned over what he gave up to marry you."

The cryptic words jolted Summer like a shock of electricity. "What he gave up to marry me?"

"Paris," Brenda said matter-of-factly.

What on earth could she be talking about? "Paris? What does that mean?"

They exchanged long, puzzled glances while Summer waited for an answer, and finally understanding dawned in Brenda's eyes. "Oh," she said, her gaze widening. "Oh my God." She covered her mouth with her hand.

"Oh my God what?"

"You don't know. He never told you. Oh, Summer, I'm so sorry."

Okay, Summer thought, what on earth was the big secret here? Would Brenda just spill it already and end the suspense? Summer's chest tightened with a curiosity that bordered on dread. "Never told me what?"

"Summer," Brenda said, "I can't believe he hasn't told you this himself, so I really feel like I'm sticking my nose in where it doesn't belong, but Brett was slated to go to Paris for a year and design a building with a famous French architect. The man selected Brett for the job himself, and it was the opportunity of a lifetime really, a chance to make a big leap in his career, from the way he explained it. When he found out you were expecting, though, he turned down the job."

Summer didn't know what to say. Her entire body felt numb. Brett had given up the opportunity of a lifetime...for her? And he'd not even consulted her about it? "I...I had no idea," she breathed.

"I tried to get him to reconsider," Brenda said, "but he told me that staying here and marrying you was the right thing to do."

"The right thing to do," Summer uttered in disbelief.

"Wait," Brenda said, reaching out to touch Summer's knee. "I didn't say that the best way. He really does love you, Summer. But he did have to turn down the job because of it."

Brenda's tone couldn't have been kinder now, yet Summer could barely hear it. She pulled in her breath to try to keep from crying. Oh God, this couldn't be, it just couldn't. Brett had given up the dream of a lifetime for *her*? It was too impossible to fathom.

She rose from the chair, shrugging free of Brenda's touch, muttering that she had to go to the bathroom. She had to be alone. She had to try to process this information. She had to try to keep from falling apart in front of his entire family.

Once secluded in the bathroom, Summer shut the door and looked in the mirror. At her face, her eyes. At her pregnant belly. *I held him back.* The words kept hammering at her heart and through her head, the only coherent thought her brain could muster at the moment.

He'd had an opportunity to further his career, an opportunity to see the world and do something important, and she'd kept him from it. It was that simple, and that horrible. He'd sacrificed his dreams for her!

She thought immediately of those heartbreaking days when it had become clear that her dreams of design school in New York were dying, that the only thing she'd ever really wanted was being taken away from her forever. And she knew in an instant she couldn't let that happen to Brett; she couldn't let him surrender his ambitions that easily.

She didn't know what she would do or how she would do it, but she refused to be the cause of his lost dreams.

7

SUMMER LAY IN BED in the dark, watching Brett sleep. She watched the way the shadows fell across his face, framing his peaceful expression. She listened to him breathe.

Part of her brimmed with love for him, with a love so great she'd never experienced anything like it. She knew it had the power to consume her, something she'd almost consented to, but she had to get her self-control back now. She'd surrendered too much to him and it had made her blind.

That forced her to think of the other part of her, the part that was so angry with him she could hardly think straight. How could he not have told her what he was giving up? Hadn't pledging their love to each other meant being honest? Hadn't it meant sharing decisions, both great and small? Summer had thought that's what it was all about—she'd even been willing to give up control of her life to have that—but maybe she'd been wrong. Apparently she'd been wrong about a lot of things.

A pang of guilt shot through her as the news Brenda had shared assaulted her all over again. Days had passed since she'd found out about Brett's job in Paris— it was now July—and still the thought of it had the ability to wound her. She supposed it just hit a little too close to home, reminded her a little too much of her own long-ago losses.

She rolled onto her back and closed her eyes, trying to shut out the memories, but instead the total darkness seemed to encourage them. Her heart still tightened when she remembered the day her father had asked her not to go to New York, but, instead, stay at home and take care of her mother. She'd seen it coming, yet she'd not really let herself believe it was going to happen. She'd kept waiting for some miracle to occur that would change everything: her mother's health, her own doomed future. She'd spent weeks hiding her tears behind schoolbooks, closed doors, whatever was handy, all the while trying to reconcile her desire to go to New York with the guilt that came at wanting to leave her ill mother behind. Not to mention the helplessness of having no choice in the matter, really. It had been a lot for an eighteen-year-old girl to handle. Even *now*, she thought, struggling to hold back familiar tears, remembering it was a lot to handle.

For a long time afterward, Summer had felt empty inside, as if she had nothing without her dream. She'd spent her whole life waiting to grow up and be a fashion designer, and suddenly she'd had nothing to look forward to, no goal to achieve. In the end, she'd discovered something she was good at, something she found fulfilling, but it had taken a long time. And she still experienced pangs of envy when the new season catalogs came out, found herself wishing, dreaming that her designs might appear inside.

Now, because of her, Brett had given up *his* dream. How could she live with that?

She opened her eyes and turned again to watch him sleep. In her mind, she saw him painting the baby's room, rubbing her pregnant belly, reading his own personal baby book by lamplight in her living room. He was a good man, such a good man...yet it all made sense to Summer now.

From the beginning, he'd been wrapped up in worrying about the baby's welfare. Sure, he'd later told her that he loved her, but when he'd first proposed, it had been about the baby, pure and simple. He'd wanted his child to have a normal family life.

Yes, he was concerned when Summer was tired or working too hard, but that was about the baby, too. Oh, she knew he cared for her, perhaps even a lot, but... maybe he didn't really care in the way you were *supposed* to care, not in the way she'd come to care about— to *love*—him.

She didn't think he'd lied about loving her—Brett was not a liar—but knowing how important the baby was to him, and hearing Brenda remind her of the importance family held for him, as well, it was suddenly easy to envision Brett *convincing* himself that he loved her, making himself believe it. The fact that Summer had no family of her own had probably made it even easier for that to happen—he'd felt sorry for her.

Brett, I know about Paris and I want you to go. I'll wait for you. I'll be here when you get back. She'd practiced saying those words over and over, yet she found too many reasons not to. The memory of Brett's persistence in the beginning hadn't faded, and she knew it would take far more than her good intentions to make him go to Paris. Besides, no matter how much he might love their child, it wasn't fair to him to be married to her if he didn't love her in that deep down forever kind of way. They'd both regret it in the end.

She'd considered talking to Tina about this when they'd gone shopping for maternity clothes just yesterday, but had decided not to. For one thing, Summer had never been good at sharing deep, personal things with anyone, so it seemed like too much of a challenge to suddenly start now. And for another, she could pretty much imagine the way the conversation would go.

"I have to end this with Brett. I have to make him follow his dream." Then she'd tell Tina exactly how she intended to accomplish that.

Tina's eyes would get as big as pancakes and her mouth would drop open. "Are you insane, Summer? Have you lost your mind? You have, haven't you? You've gone completely bonkers."

Summer shook her head in the darkness. No, Tina would never understand. *No one* would. No one who hadn't been through the kind of loss she had, the kind of loss Brett was about to experience if she didn't turn the tables.

Summer took a deep breath, then lay back on her pillow. There was no decision involved, but simply this thing she would have to do now.

She wouldn't let him sacrifice his dream job for her. He was going to Paris if it killed her—and it probably would—but that was beside the point. She knew he was too gentlemanly and sweet to go unless he felt forced to, so that's what she would have to do, force him out of her life.

She'd been right all along. When you love somebody, you make sacrifices for them. Brett loved their baby and he had sacrificed his career. Now, because Summer loved him, she was going to sacrifice her own happiness for his future.

She was going to give him up, no matter how hard it would be.

SUMMER CALLED Foster-Hardin at quarter past twelve the following day.

"Hi, Anna," she said merrily, "it's Summer. Is Brett in, or is he at lunch?" Luckily, she'd talked to Anna on the phone several times and had even met her once.

"Oh, I'm sorry, you just missed him. He and Mr. Foster are meeting with clients at LaNormandie and I don't expect them back until after two. But I'd be happy to call the restaurant if it's anything urgent."

Perfect, Summer thought. Prime snooping time. "No, Anna, nothing urgent," she said, "but I may stop by the office anyway. I think we got some of our work files mixed up at my place last night, so I'd like to take a look for them."

"I can do that for you if you like," Anna said. "It might save you the trouble of coming over here."

"No," Summer said, hoping she wasn't too abrupt. "I don't mind looking myself. I don't have any lunch plans and I could use the walk. My doctor says I need to start getting some exercise, so it'll be good for me."

She could practically hear Anna smiling over the phone—her ploy to distract her with female-bonding type things had worked. "Well then, I'll see you soon," Anna said.

Luckily, the Foster-Hardin office was quiet when Summer arrived—lunchtime had emptied the place out. "Hi, Mrs. Ford," Anna greeted her, then immediately slapped her hand over her mouth. "I'm so sorry," she said, wide-eyed and blushing. "I don't know why I did that. I guess I've just been talking to Brett so much about your upcoming wedding that I..." She smiled. "Well, I guess you'll be Mrs. Ford soon enough, won't you?"

Summer's stomach nearly dropped as the younger woman stammered over her blunder. *Mrs. Ford.* Summer loved the sound of that. She couldn't believe how *much* she loved it—it sounded so right. But it was all wrong and she'd have to quit loving it just as quickly as she'd started.

She worked very hard to return the smile. "You *could* just call me Summer, you know. No need to be formal."

Anna seemed touched by the suggestion. "Okay then, Summer it is. How're you feeling?" she asked, motioning to Summer's tummy.

"Quite good, actually," Summer replied, still wearing a pasted-on smile. "I had morning sickness for a while, but it's been gone for weeks." She found it difficult to keep acting happy, but she had to pretend well if she were to pull this off.

Now it was time to ply Anna for information. Summer started toward Brett's office, then stopped and looked back as if a thought had just struck her. "Oh, Anna, I was trying to remember—what's the name of that architect in Paris? The one Brett was going to work with?"

"Andre Bruseaux," Anna replied.

"That's right," Summer said, snapping her fingers. "I was telling someone about him this morning and his name slipped my mind."

Moments later, Summer had found Andre Bruseaux's phone number in Brett's address book. Jotting it down, she stuffed it in her purse, returned to the office lobby and thanked Anna for her help as she waited for the elevator.

"Did you find what you needed?" Anna asked.

"Absolutely," Summer replied, hoping, as the elevator doors closed behind her, that Anna hadn't noticed she wasn't carrying any folders.

After walking the few blocks back to Stafford's, Summer made her way to her office, where she shut the door, sat down behind the desk, then dialed the international phone number.

Two receptionists and much nervousness later, she heard a deep, French-accented voice say, "Andre Bruseaux."

Summer took a deep breath before she spoke—everything hinged on how well she handled this conversation. "Mr. Bruseaux, my name is Mary Peterson and I'm a business reporter for the *Cincinnati Enquirer* in the United States."

Mr. Bruseaux stayed disturbingly quiet, so Summer plodded on.

"I'm doing an article on the architectural firm of Foster-Hardin, featuring their up-and-coming associate, Brett Ford."

"Mr. Ford is a fine young architect," Mr. Bruseaux said, and Summer was relieved to have caught his attention with Brett's name.

"I understand Mr. Ford recently declined an opportunity to work with you in Paris."

"That's true."

"Well—" here went nothing "—sources tell me that Mr. Ford's circumstances may soon change and that he may have a renewed interest in going to Europe."

"Is that so?"

"Yes, it is." Summer swallowed hard before going on. "Can you tell me, Mr. Bruseaux, if you've filled that position yet?"

"No, I have not," Mr. Bruseaux said. "Mr. Ford was my first choice, and when he originally accepted, I saw no need to look further. Since he declined, I've had no luck finding anyone else whose work impressed me as his did."

"So if Mr. Ford decided to come to Paris, after all, the job would still be his?"

"Certainly. Now, tell me, what do you know about his change of circumstance, Miss..."

Summer had to think for a second to summon the reporter's name. "Peterson."

"Miss Peterson, what makes you think Mr. Ford will change his mind?"

"Well," she said, hoping she wasn't going to cross the lines of professionalism and drive Bruseaux away, "I'm told that Mr. Ford declined the job for personal reasons, namely an unexpected engagement. But I understand that things aren't working out, that he and his fiancée may soon split. If that happens, there would likely be nothing to stand in the way of his coming to Paris."

"Hmm, that's most interesting," Mr. Bruseaux mused. "You seem quite attuned to Mr. Ford's personal life, Miss Peterson."

That was putting it mildly, Summer thought. She feared she sounded more like a Hollywood gossip columnist than an earnest journalist. "Yes, well, I *am* a reporter," she replied lamely. "We *are* rather known for...sticking our noses into other people's business."

"How candid of you," Mr. Bruseaux observed.

"At any rate," Summer said, wanting desperately to get back to the subject, "I think if you were to call Mr. Ford in, say, a few weeks, you might find him quite receptive to your offer."

"And how exactly does this benefit *you*?"

Summer scrambled for an answer. "Well," she said, "a local architect setting off for fame and fortune in Paris makes a much more interesting story than one who is not."

"I see," Mr. Bruseaux said, seeming to buy it.

"I thank you for your time," she said quickly, then hung up the phone, about to burst. She leaned back in her chair, her heart beating a mile a minute.

She couldn't believe what she'd just done, but she'd had no choice.

Step one in repairing Brett's dream was complete. Now on to the really hard part—step two.

SUMMER BRACED HERSELF as she turned the doorknob. Stepping into the quiet house, she felt her stomach churn as she moved toward the dim light that shone from a lamp in the living room. This was the third night in a row she'd worked late, and it was the third night in a row Brett had specifically asked her not to.

She'd done it on purpose, even though she'd have actually rather been at home with him, snuggled up inside the house he thought they would soon officially share. It had been the only way she could think of to trigger the beginning of the end.

She stopped in the foyer, not quite ready to face him. She knew he was waiting for her on the sofa, in the soft lamplight, undoubtedly wearing a familiar, wounded look in his eyes.

That meant her plan was working, of course, but how would she stand it? How would she manage not to cave in? How could she continue hurting him like this?

The answers to those questions didn't really matter, though, she just knew she had to do it. In the end, he would be happy, fulfilled, and that made it right. She forged ahead into the room, prepared to do imaginary battle with her fiancée.

She found him brooding handsomely, elbow propped on the arm of the sofa, stubbled chin resting in his hand. He turned toward her, his eyes dark with the pain she'd expected but still wasn't quite prepared for. Like the last time she'd decided to do battle with Brett, it wasn't as easy as she'd anticipated. She swallowed heavily and even took a step back. *Be strong,* she told herself. *You can do this. You have to.*

She ignored the crumbling of her heart as she set down her briefcase and slipped off her shoes. "Dinner?" she asked casually.

"I already ate," he told her. "I cooked, and since you said you'd be home by six, that's when it was ready. Leftovers are in the fridge," he added, drawing his gaze away.

Summer didn't have to glance at her watch to know it was nearly eight o'clock. She felt just as guilty as she should have, but she couldn't let it show. Instead, she'd have to provoke him further. "So you're mad," she said.

"Well, yeah, I am. Six usually means six."

"Sorry," she said, clearly without meaning it. "I had a lot of work to do."

"Of course," he continued as if he hadn't heard her, "six usually means six, but on Tuesday it meant seven, last night it meant seven-thirty and tonight it apparently means eight."

"You know how important my job is to me, Brett," she said harshly, welcoming his anger and falsely returning it.

"Yeah, I know that," he said, "but I was under the impression that we'd come to an understanding, that during the pregnancy you'd cut back on the late hours to take care of yourself and the baby. And it seemed to be working out just fine," he added, "until a few days ago."

Until I knew about Paris, Summer thought futilely, but this was no time for whining, even on the inside. She had to keep forging through this; she had to keep hold of her control. "Well, I tried," she told him.

"And it was going well."

"No, it was leaving piles of unfinished business on my desk."

"I thought you were delegating."

"Mistakes were being made," she lied. "I had to take some of the work back."

He stayed silent as he rose from his seat, his steely gaze penetrating hers. Oh God, she wished things were different, but they weren't. She stood waiting for his next argument.

When it didn't come, Summer reached for the big guns. "Is this how it's going to be after we're married? You watching my every move, expecting me to be at your beck and call?"

He tilted his head, looking at her as if she were being childish, and it embarrassed her. It *was* childish to throw such a trite, meaningless, almost threatening accusation at him. "Summer…" he finally began, his voice scolding.

But maybe her trite threat had worked? "Yes?"

"Let's not fight," he said, surprising her with his calm tone as he lifted his hand gently to her cheek. Damn it, why did he have to be so forgiving, so good-hearted? How badly she wanted to savor that touch, to step closer, to cuddle in his arms. "Listen, why don't you go change clothes and I'll get out the leftovers and heat them up for you."

Summer felt her control begin to dissolve. "You don't have to do that," she said, her voice little more than a whisper.

"I know I don't have to," he said, "but I don't wanna fight. So go change clothes, and then you can eat, and then we can…talk about things. How's that?"

More than reasonable, she thought. *Incredibly, completely* reasonable. More reasonable than she'd have imagined any man could be after the stuff she was pulling. And where was her control? It had vanished completely.

"That's fine," she said softly.

Summer padded up the stairs, her heart beating too hard. It was so easy for him to move her, to melt her resolve. Her own thought about him from months ago came back: he was her only weakness. It had proven true over and over, and it was proving true now, but she had to fight that, harder now than she ever had before. For his sake. For his happiness.

She changed into a nightgown, then slipped on a short summer robe, and as she was trying to come up with her next course of action, she spotted something new in the nursery and stepped inside.

The baby bed had arrived, the one Brett had arranged to borrow from Jackie.

Summer ran her hand over the smooth wood railing and imagined laying her little one down to sleep in it, twisting a mobile above to create tinkling music for her baby. She'd seen one she liked the other day; it had four teddy bears suspended from it and played "Rock-a-bye Baby." It occurred to her just now, looking up at the recently decorated walls, that it would match the motif in the border. She decided she'd go buy it this weekend.

And then she realized the bed had provided the next part of her plan.

It would be horribly mean, horribly unfair, and it would take a lot of heartlessness to pull it off.

But she had to. Hard as it was, she had to.

So she tightened the tie on her robe and marched down the stairs and into the dining room. Brett had reheated dinner—baked chicken, mashed potatoes and green beans. Oh God, he was sweet, and this was going to be so, so hard. Especially since he was sitting in the chair next to hers at the table, grinning the crooked grin she loved.

Control, she told herself, summoning it back. *Control.*

Summer took a very deep breath and looked into his eyes, and then she began. "What's that baby bed doing up there?"

Her tone obviously startled him, and he simply gaped at her for a minute before answering. "Remember," he said, "I told you about the bed. It's Jackie's. They were cleaning out their attic, so Tom brought it over in his truck after work today."

"Just like that?" she snapped. "Without even asking me first?"

"What do you mean, just like that? I *did* ask you. I thought we had agreed on it."

"Well, maybe I changed my mind."

He looked completely baffled, staring at her with his mouth half-open, eyes puzzled. "You changed your mind," he repeated.

"You picked out the colors without me, and the border, and the trim color. You picked out everything," she complained. "Maybe I'd like to pick out something, too."

"Wait," he said, sounding exasperated, "I told you if you didn't like it, we could redo it. I'm not trying to pick out everything, Summer, really, but I thought you liked it all, and I thought you wanted the bed. That's what you said."

Summer took a deep breath. Here came the really tough part. She could no longer look at him as she spoke, so she dropped her eyes toward the table. "You know, I didn't really want you to be a part of this at all. Remember? I wanted to have this baby alone."

The room went deadly quiet. She could have sworn she heard both of them breathing, as well as the clock ticking, each passing second adding to the tension and pain that filled the air. Her heart felt as though it were being crushed in her chest. Finally, she gathered the courage to lift her eyes to his.

"I remember," he said, his voice surprisingly soft.

Another long silence followed and Summer knew it was her move. She also knew what the move was. Now to actually make it.

This is for him, she reminded herself. *All for him, and his future. You can do it.*

"Maybe I was right in the first place," she finally said. "Maybe that's what I really wanted all along. Maybe it's what I *still* want. To have this baby alone."

Brett just looked at her. She tried to read his eyes, but couldn't. She saw him swallow, and thought perhaps he was about to explode with anger, when he simply began to shake his head and said, "No, I can't believe that, Summer. Not now, not after all this."

"What do you mean, you can't believe it?"

"I love you and you love me," he reminded her. "You don't want to have the baby alone. I know you don't."

"How many times do I have to explain to you, Brett," she said, falling back on an old, faithful standard, "that I can't let anyone else control me? And that's exactly what's happened here. I've let you begin to control my life, control my time, control my decisions, and I don't like it."

"Then we'll talk about it some more, love," he said, reaching out to touch her arm with gentle fingertips. He'd called her *love!* It moved her to the depths of her soul, made her love him so much she could barely breathe. "We'll talk about it and we'll compromise and we'll do whatever we have to do to work it out. Now relax and eat your dinner. Take it easy. Okay?"

Oh, damn him for being so reasonable. This was killing her, but at least he'd just provided her with more ammunition. "Quit telling me what to do," she snapped.

And then it happened—Brett finally fell off the edge she'd been pushing him toward. "Damn it, Summer, you're not making any sense here! I'm breaking my back trying to be understanding and do the right thing, but you won't cut me any slack! What do you want from me?"

"I want you to leave me alone!" she screamed.

He glared at her. "You want to be left alone? Fine! I'll leave you alone!" He stormed from the room, and Summer listened, her heart beating a mile a minute, as the front door slammed behind him.

Sweet success. Ironically, it brought a tear to her eye.

Numb, she lowered herself into her chair and began to eat her dinner, the wonderful home-cooked meal Brett had made for her. Too bad she'd just lost her appetite.

BRETT FELT THINGS falling apart. He didn't know why it was happening; he couldn't explain it, especially after the glorious weeks of happiness they'd shared just before the trouble had begun. Yet it seemed that no matter what he did or said, Summer found fault with him.

He drummed his fingertips on the arm of the chair in the waiting room. Where was Summer *now?* He'd gotten used to her being late from work, but was she going to be late for her doctor's appointment, too?

He shook his head in irritation. What was going on with her lately? He'd even been tempted to call Tina and ask her about Summer, but he'd decided they should be able to work out their problems without pulling in help from outside. Of course, it would be a lot easier to solve those problems if Summer would give him even an inch. He tried to be patient, tried to be fair, tried to offer alternatives to her concerns, but nothing worked. And he tried his damnedest to hold his anger inside, yet sometimes it was beyond him to do that. He'd never been so frustrated in his life.

It wasn't only petty arguments keeping them apart, either. Just last night, Brett had gently wrapped himself around her in bed and begun raining soft kisses on her neck. She'd squirmed against him and he hadn't known if that meant he should stop or go on. When he'd moved his hand to her breast, though, she'd made her intentions clear by pushing it away.

"You don't want to make love?" he'd whispered in her ear.

"No."

It was the fourth consecutive night he'd met with refusal. "How come?"

"It's…getting on in the pregnancy," she'd said.

Yet he knew better than that—he was an educated daddy-to-be. "It's not even *close* to too late, Summer. But if you want, we can do it like this, from behind, like we're supposed to at the end," he'd said, then rubbed himself teasingly against her.

For a strange, lingering moment, he'd felt something like acquiescence in the air, and he'd been almost sure she would change her mind. He'd sensed her wanting him.

But it was not to be. "Brett," she'd whispered, her voice going harsh, "I said no. Now let's go to sleep."

Lately, he'd even been wondering why he still slept at

her house, let alone tried to make love to her. Everything between them had grown strained, and he often had the distinct feeling she didn't want him there. Still, going back to his apartment, after her place had started feeling so much like *their* place, seemed like giving up, like a defeat he couldn't bear to let happen. Besides, he'd already returned his keys to Mrs. Greenbaum; it had seemed silly to keep the apartment for another couple of weeks when there was nothing in it anymore. He'd moved his whole life to Summer's house.

The front door of the doctor's office opened and a pregnant woman walked in, but it wasn't the one he was waiting for. He checked his watch. Three forty-five. She was fifteen minutes late for the appointment. What could be keeping her? Should he call and see if she'd left work yet? Was it possible that she might even have forgotten?

Brett released a long sigh and was just about to go verify the appointment time with the receptionist when the office's inner door opened, and who came through it but Summer.

"See you next time," a cheery woman in medical scrubs said behind her.

Brett simply stared in disbelief. His eyes met Summer's as he rose from the chair, but neither of them said a word.

She looked...defiant. He hated that look. He'd gotten so used to, and attached to, the softer Summer, the woman he'd fallen in love with, and he had a bad feeling about what was coming. But he didn't say anything until they reached the parking lot.

"What's going on?" he asked pointedly once they were outside.

She cast her eyes toward the hot pavement at first,

then boldly lifted her gaze. "I rescheduled the appointment for three instead of three-thirty."

She'd rescheduled the appointment? That made no sense. "Why?" he fumed. "And why didn't you tell me? You knew I wanted to be there."

"*That's* why," she said, a hot wind lifting her hair. "Because I *didn't* want you there."

Brett took a deep breath. He pushed back the hurt that surged through his veins, because there were more important issues here than that one. "Why not?" he asked, struggling to keep his voice quiet.

Her eyes narrowed, somehow deepening her obstinate expression, and whatever breeze had existed a moment ago now vanished completely. "Because this is about me," she said, "and my baby. *My* baby, Brett."

"My baby, too," he reminded her sharply.

"Only by chance," she replied.

Brett couldn't quite believe she'd just said that. "What the hell is that supposed to mean?"

"What do you think it means? It means that we met one night, we went to bed together and I got pregnant. This is not a child conceived in love, Brett. Never was."

"That doesn't make it any less my child," he told her, "and it doesn't mean I don't love you now."

He watched her closely, trying somehow to read her, but digging beneath that tough facade was impossible. It reminded him of the cool personality he'd encountered that first night at Dunbar's, the one that had warned him to stay away.

Her lips began to tremble and he longed to take her hands in his, but he was afraid, afraid to do anything, afraid that whatever he chose, it would be wrong.

"Let's just talk about it after we get home," she said.

Then, without casting him a second glance, she walked away, got into her car and drove from the parking lot.

BRETT COULDN'T even remember the drive to Summer's house. "Home," she'd called it. *Whose* home? he suddenly wondered.

He loved her, damn it, and he was pretty sure she loved him, too...or it had certainly seemed that way for a while. Yet suddenly nothing they'd shared seemed to matter to her. He couldn't make sense of it, regardless of how he tried, and his blood boiled as he remembered the things she'd just said to him outside the doctor's office.

Sure, once upon a time this had been primarily about the baby, about the happy, normal family life he wanted his child to have, but that had changed. Now it was about her and their life together, and the idea that he might be losing her tore him up inside.

What had happened to the Summer he'd fallen in love with, the Summer he'd thought had fallen in love with him? It was as if she'd been invaded by a body snatcher or something. Without warning, in the blink of an eye, everything had changed.

Once inside the house, Brett found her sitting in the living room, her stockinged feet lifted to rest on the coffee table.

"What did the doctor say?" he asked, taking a seat next to her on the sofa. "Everything all right with the baby?"

"Yes," she said without looking at him, "the baby's fine."

"So then," he continued, deciding they might as well get on with it, "are you ready to talk about what you said back there in the parking lot?"

"Yes," she said. "I've been doing a lot of thinking, Brett, and I've decided this isn't working."

Her words took his breath away. *What* wasn't working? *Them?* Brett feared his worst nightmare was about to be played out before his eyes and that nothing he could do would stop it.

At least he could try, though. "It was working fine until a week ago when you started going ballistic at every turn."

"It isn't working out," she repeated, "and I don't want to pretend anymore."

Brett's chest tightened and it got even harder to breathe. "What exactly are you saying, Summer?"

He saw her swallow. She still didn't look at him. "I'm saying I want you to leave."

He had almost anticipated it, but it still struck him like a blow to the gut. "Leave?"

"Yes."

It wasn't the first time she'd asked him to leave. It seemed her way of punctuating every argument. Yet this time the command sounded more serious than ever before. "Are you saying you want to break off the engagement?" he asked. "Call off the wedding?"

Her breathing was slow and trembly. "Just go," she said.

This couldn't be happening. Summer was asking him to leave the home they'd begun to build together—really leave. "Summer, answer me. Are you calling off our wedding?"

She took a deep breath. "Yes."

He'd seen it coming, of course—he'd insisted she say it—but that didn't keep it from feeling like she'd just crushed his heart in a vise. "Summer, I love you. I don't want to call things off. I don't want to leave."

"You love our baby," she said, "which is fine. I'll deal with that, but you and I are...incompatible. I did what you asked me. I tried to give up my independence and I tried to compromise. I tried to share my life. But I'm tired of trying. It's not working out for me. So please don't argue with me, all right?"

"No, it's not all right! I won't give up this easily!"

"You don't have a choice. This is my house—"

"It was becoming *our* house."

"This is *my* house and I want you out of it! Now!"

Brett sat before her dumbfounded. When had they started yelling? How had things turned so ugly? "You're serious?" he finally asked.

She gave a terse nod. She still hadn't looked him in the eye.

"Look at me and say it, Summer," he told her. "Look at me and tell me you really want me to leave...for good."

A long silence stretched between them. She sat as still as stone, her gaze focused straight before her. He began to wonder if she was weakening somehow, and a glimmer of hope actually fought its way into his heart.

Yet then she slowly turned to face him and their eyes met. "I really want you to leave, Brett. For good."

A knife couldn't have sliced deeper into his soul. His body went limp. She really wanted to end their engagement, their relationship—everything. He looked at her a moment more, felt a certain numbness set in, then rose and went upstairs.

He grabbed the garment bag he used for business travel and stuffed a couple of suits and dress shirts inside. Then he grabbed a duffel bag and threw in some jeans and shorts and T-shirts. He moved quickly, so his momentum wouldn't die.

When he was done, he took his bags downstairs and

walked out of Summer's house without even looking at her again. It was the only way he could actually make himself go.

SUMMER LISTENED to the door slam. It had been slammed a lot over the past week or so—by both of them. Only this time it was different; this time Brett wasn't coming back.

She sat on the couch and took deep gulps, trying to get air to her lungs. Then the deep gulps began to be mixed with tears, combining until she was racked with sobs, sobs filled with all the pain and emptiness that coursed through her veins as if it would never stop.

Oh God, she'd sent him away. She'd really made him go. And...calling off the wedding? Yes, that's what she'd intended, but when he'd said the words, it had almost paralyzed her. All she really knew was that she wanted him to go to Paris, wanted him to reach his dreams, no matter how cruel she had to be to make him do it.

When the sobbing subsided, she lay her head back on the couch and felt new tears roll down over her temples to dampen her hair. It had been a hell of a week with all the fighting, all the coldness, all the warm, loving touches she'd pushed away. How many times had she been close to giving in? Too, too many. And too many times she had wanted to tell him, *I love you, this is all a big mistake, I don't mean anything I'm saying.*

Still, she'd stood firm. Step two was complete now.

And Summer was completely heartbroken. She'd succeeded in driving the father of her child and the man she loved out of her life. But she'd had to do it, because she loved him.

Now Brett could have the life he was *meant* to have. He could follow his dreams without having her stand in his way.

8

SUMMER LAY IN BED, watching the way the sunlight filtered through the curtains. It was four in the afternoon and she'd come home early, feeling tired and worn. Partially because of the pregnancy and partially, she knew, because of how much she missed Brett. They were supposed to have gotten married this weekend, but the elegant white dress she'd chosen would still hang in her closet when Monday morning came, and the hankie Brett's mom had embroidered with the date of their wedding would become a useless reminder of all the happiness they'd never share.

Summer had known having him leave would be hard, but she hadn't realized it would be *this* hard. She'd never been so depressed in her life, not even when she'd had to give up design school.

Oddly, everything she'd believed about having control over her life had turned out to be entirely false. She'd liked coming home to him. She'd liked sleeping next to him. She didn't even really mind him insisting that she leave work at a decent hour; in the time since he'd been gone, she'd even started doing that on her own. Today, for instance, she'd come home early, and the universe hadn't come to an end—it had been no big deal. The big deal had been coming home to an empty house.

Memories of him lingered everywhere, as he'd not yet

picked up the rest of his things. She saw him in the un-done crossword puzzles in the newspaper every night, she saw him in the architectural books he'd left behind in the bookcase, and she was completely surrounded by him every time she walked into the nursery, the room he'd so lovingly prepared for their baby. She hadn't re-alized how fully Brett had penetrated her life, how much a part of her world he'd become, but it was true. He'd become the biggest part of her very quickly, and now that he was gone, she felt like an empty shell.

Susan had called Summer after the big blowup to try to get to the bottom of things, and Summer had been forced to spin the same lies to her that she had to Brett. Lying to the woman she'd come to think of as a friend had been almost as hard as lying to Brett himself. What must his family think of her now? Especially after hav-ing to cancel the extravagant wedding they'd gone to such lengths to plan for her. Well, it wouldn't do any good to brood over that. At least now Brett could have his career—as soon as Andre Bruseaux called him.

Summer rolled over in bed and looked at the pillow Brett had slept on while he'd been there. She'd fluffed it and flipped it a hundred times, trying to change the shape of it somehow, trying to make it seem like a new pillow that had never been used before, but the pillow made her think of Brett, too.

Getting sleepy, she closed her eyes and let herself imagine that he was there next to her, close to her, let herself imagine that she might reach out and touch him at any moment. Even if she couldn't have him anymore, she couldn't keep herself from wanting him there. Feel-ing almost as if she could take in the scent of him, as if she could breathe him in, she drifted into sleep.

BRETT LEFT THE OFFICE early and headed home to his parents' house, where he was staying for now, since he'd given up his apartment too soon. He'd planned to start looking for a new apartment tonight, or maybe a condo—he wanted a place big enough for the baby to have his own room when he was there, and plenty of space to play—but at the moment, apartment hunting had moved to the back of his mind. Something important had happened today: Andre Bruseaux had called and asked him to reconsider taking the job in Paris.

Brett couldn't have been more surprised to hear Bruseaux's voice, and his surprise had grown as Bruseaux had gone on about still wanting him for the job. The call had been the first thing to lift his spirits since Summer had thrown him out of her house and her life, and despite himself, a part of him was tempted to take the job and just get the hell out of here for a while.

Of course, Anna had taken the call before patching it through to him, and she'd wasted no time in flitting down the hall to tell Mr. Foster. The whole office knew his engagement had fallen apart, and Mr. Foster had come to his office right after Brett hung up the phone, reminding him that this was a rare second chance of a lifetime.

Brett still harbored some heavy doubts, though. Even if Summer didn't want to give their relationship a go, he still had the baby to consider. He wanted to be there for his son each step of the way, from the beginning.

So he had some serious thinking to do.

He went inside the house, kissed his mother on the cheek and changed into casual clothes. When he headed right back toward the front door, she said, "You just got home. Where are you going already?"

"It's early, so I thought it'd be a good time to get some

of my stuff from Summer's house." Actually, the idea had just occurred to him. Whether he was going to Paris or just buying a condo, the time had come to abide by Summer's wishes and clear out of her life completely, which meant getting the rest of his belongings. And the timing was right. Besides the fact that she wouldn't be home at this hour, the decision about Paris might help keep his mind occupied and prevent him from dwelling on his heartache.

His mother rewarded him with a solemn nod that said, *I know how much you're hurting, but I won't make you talk about it.* And he was glad. Things were hard enough as it was right now.

He knew he should have already gotten the rest of his things, yet he hadn't wanted to risk bumping into Summer. He still loved the woman, but she'd made it more than clear that she didn't desire his presence. A guy could argue with that only so much. He didn't know what would happen when the baby came, how they'd manage to deal with that, but for now, he thought it was best to do what she wanted. He didn't know what other choice he even had.

It hurt pulling into her driveway, which had already begun feeling like *his* driveway. It hurt to slip the key into the lock and step inside the place he'd started to think of as home. But he'd be quick about it, in and out.

He swiftly packed some of his books in a duffel bag he'd brought, then he decided to go upstairs and start cleaning out the closet she'd given him.

On the way to the bedroom, he stopped and peeked into the nursery. She hadn't gotten a new baby bed yet, but the colorful walls reminded him of the time they'd spent together putting on the finishing touches. He hoped the baby would enjoy the room as much as he'd enjoyed getting it ready. *But this is no time to linger,* he reminded himself, *no time to dwell on the past, or the future that will no longer be. Just get your stuff and get out.*

When he stepped into Summer's bedroom, though, Brett was jolted to a halt. Summer lay on the bed in a thin white nightgown, looking almost angelic. Her eyes fluttered open and met his immediately.

He felt the instant need to defend himself. "I came to get my stuff. I didn't think you'd be here."

"I came home early," she said, her voice gentle and containing not a hint of bitterness.

"Is anything wrong? Are you sick?"

She shook her head against the pillow. "Just a little tired."

"I'm glad you came home then."

She released a tiny breath and reached for her pregnant belly.

"What is it?" he asked. "Does something hurt?"

"No," she said. To his surprise, the expression on her face was actually pleasant, peaceful. "It's just the baby kicking."

The news took him aback. "The baby is kicking? Really?" He'd been waiting for this to happen; he remembered thinking about it back when her pregnancy had been brand-new. But now, knowing that it was really, finally happening...well, it seemed amazing.

She treated him to a soft smile, a smile he'd missed so much that this one felt like it reached all the way to his soul. "Yeah," she said. "I felt it once the other day. This is only the second time."

He took a hesitant step toward her, then stopped. "Can I—I mean..."

He watched her take a deep breath, saw her considering his unspoken request. "Yes," she said finally. "You can feel."

He moved cautiously forward, still a bit in disbelief that their baby was so...*human* in there that he had little feet that could kick. Brett had felt each of his sisters' babies kick, but this, his *own* baby kicking, stunned him in a marvelous way.

He knelt beside the bed and lifted tentative fingers toward her. Taking his hand, she placed it on the growing mound of her belly. "Here," she said.

A moment later he felt it, a tiny movement from inside. "Wow," he murmured, meeting Summer's gaze.

When the baby kicked again, this one coming a little harder, Brett widened his eyes in awe. "Oh wow," he said, louder this time.

As he and Summer looked at each other, he didn't see any of the coldness that had framed their relationship, beginning and end. He only saw the sweet eyes of the woman he'd fallen in love with. It was a perfect moment—him and her, experiencing some sense of harmony. And the baby, too...the baby living inside her, the baby he'd made with her, moving against his hand.

"Hey, little guy," he said, leaning toward her belly. "This is your dad, buddy. I can't wait to meet you. It won't be long now."

Then, on impulse, he leaned over and gave the baby a little kiss through Summer's gauzy gown, as he had once before, back when they were happy. She didn't protest, so he very gently rested his cheek against her there, thinking how incredible that she and the baby were one right now, that he could almost touch the baby by touching her.

A moment later, he lowered another tiny kiss in the

same spot as before. Though this kiss, too, was meant for the baby, it was also sort of like kissing Summer.

And she wasn't protesting.

He kissed her again, this time higher on her belly, dropping a gentle hand to her hip. He sensed her drawing in her breath...and still not protesting. At all.

When his kiss rose to her breast, she trembled beneath him. Swallowed hard. Still did not protest. Brett surged with the warmth of wanting her, of being wanted by her.

He stayed painstakingly tender, sprinkling baby kisses on her throat, her neck, her cheek. He was afraid to look into her eyes, but when he did, he found her expression timid yet wanting, and he fell in love with her all over again.

"I love you," he breathed. She didn't answer, and he hadn't expected her to, but she still said nothing to make him stop.

He dropped more gentle kisses over her eyelids, her nose, finally her lips. Sweet, soft kisses that she met with a barely discernible pressure that made all the difference in the world to Brett.

"I want to make love to you," he whispered in her ear. She said nothing, yet released a trembling sigh that Brett knew meant yes.

Brett climbed onto the bed, rolling himself behind her, wrapping his arms carefully around her. He tenderly cupped one breast in his hand, raining still more soft kisses on her neck. She sighed.

Slowly, he reached down and slid his hand beneath her nightgown, barely grazing her thigh with the slow ascent of his fingertips. When he began to pull down her panties, she lifted to help him, and when they were gone, he unzipped his shorts.

Carefully then, he slid inside her.

She released a tiny gasp.

"Hurt?" he whispered.

"No," she whispered back. "No."

Summer knew this was wrong. She knew it negated everything, every step she'd made toward helping him achieve his goals.

But she'd been dreaming of him, and then she'd opened her eyes and found him there. He'd been kissing her so sweetly, too sweetly to resist, and now he was inside her, deep inside her, filling her, filling the emptiness, soothing her every pain. She'd been powerless to say no, and as before—as always—Brett had once again proven to be her greatest weakness.

Now he was whispering to her—wonderful, precious words. "I've missed you...I've missed *this*. You're so beautiful.... This feels so right, Summer, so good and so right." His breath in her ear warmed her nearly as much as his lovemaking, slow and deep and intense and beyond anything she'd ever experienced before. Summer had no choice but to give herself up to it, to the moment, to the deep flood of sensation. To lose herself in him, just for now. Just for a little while.

Brett couldn't wait much longer. He'd gone very slow, but he'd missed her so much, needed her so badly. When he shuddered and gave himself over to his body's need for release, the thick, heavy waves washed over him, swallowed him, finally drained him and left him in that warm resting place that came after.

He leaned into her, pressing against her back, and she clutched tight to the hand he wrapped around her body. Holding her, he fell into the most peaceful sleep he'd experienced since they'd been apart.

WHEN SUMMER WOKE, things were surreal. Dream and reality had gotten dangerously mixed together. Oh God, what had she done? She'd made love to him! And as always, it had been stupendous.

But damn it, what now?

She shifted in his arms, realizing it was a place she shouldn't be, and he gently rolled her onto her back, their eyes meeting. His were tentative, tender. She wanted to cry at the love she saw in them.

"Do you still want me to go?" he whispered.

Come on, Summer, you have to do this. Do it right. End it now.

Yet she just couldn't be mean this time. She had to make him understand some other way. "You have to, Brett," she said softly.

"We were supposed to get married tomorrow. You know that, don't you?"

She gave a silent nod.

"It's not too late, Summer," he told her. "We could still do it. I still want to be your husband."

"It *is* too late," she insisted.

"Tell me why."

Her heart fluttered painfully. "Because," she began, "I just don't want to marry you."

She watched him draw in his breath, and hated herself for her words.

"I just...wasn't happy. " She forced herself to go on, struggling to keep her voice calm. "I'm sure it's hard for you to understand why things changed, but they just did. I can't help it. I've spent my whole life not wanting to be married, and I still don't."

"What about making love?" he whispered.

"Making love is good," she answered, "but it's..." Oh God, could she really say this? "It's only sex."

Summer couldn't look at him anymore because she'd just dealt a horrible blow, no matter how gently she'd said it. And now, although she knew she would hate herself for this later, she was going to end this once and for all by doing the most heartless, brutal thing she could think of. "The truth is, Brett...I don't love you."

Instinct made her risk a glance at him, regretfully. He looked like she'd just ripped his heart from his chest. Maybe she had. Damn it, she had to finish this.

"I tried, Brett, the whole time we were engaged, I tried. But despite what I may have said or how I may have acted, I just...don't...love you. And even for the sake of the child, I can't be married to a man I don't love."

There, it was out now. The most terrible lie she'd ever told. Her chest hurt and she wanted to cry, but she'd said it.

Brett gently withdrew from her and rose from the bed. His movements seemed slow but fluid. After he'd zipped up his shorts, he reached in his pocket and laid a key on the dresser, the key to her house, she presumed. With his back to her, he said, "I'll send someone for my things on Saturday." Then he walked from the room.

Summer waited until she heard the front door close downstairs. She waited until she heard him start his car, back it from the driveway and pull away. Then she let the floodgates open. Heavy tears rolled down her face and waves of sobs began to shake her mercilessly.

She'd sent him away again, she'd broken his heart in the process and she knew he wouldn't be back this time.

This was what you wanted, she reminded herself.

Hard to believe.

Yet then she remembered the goal of this whole thing

again. Let him have Paris. Let him have his career. Let him have the chances she'd never had. Let him go.

She'd done that now.

WHEN BRETT RETURNED to his parents' house, Brenda's car sat in the driveway. Damn it, he was in no mood for a chat, with her or anyone else. Unfortunately, it would be impossible to get into the house and past his sister and mother without being seen.

"Where are your things, dear?" his mother asked from the sofa when he walked in empty-handed.

"She was home," he answered simply.

He saw the two women exchange looks after his reply, and though he knew they both loved him very much, he'd grown tired of being an object of pity.

"I told her I'd send somebody over for my stuff on Saturday," he added.

"Susan and I will go," his mother offered.

He didn't argue—it was a good idea. They both liked Summer and he knew she liked them in return.

"Something else happened, too," he said, taking a seat with them in the living room. He'd decided on impulse that he might as well fill them in. Maybe it would take his mind off the horrible void in his heart. "Before I left work today, Andre Bruseaux called me. He still wants me to take the job."

He watched their eyes light up, and wished he could feel as enthusiastic. "Oh, Brett, you should take it!" Brenda said. "It would be so good for you to just forget this whole mess with Summer and go to Paris for a year. Wouldn't it, Mom?"

"Well," his mother said slowly, "it's still a wonderful opportunity, and I'll admit the timing is good."

He knew what she meant, but he still said, "Not really. What about the baby?"

"The baby isn't due until November," Brenda reminded him.

"You can make arrangements to come back after the baby is born," his mother added hopefully.

"I had planned on *being* at the hospital when the baby was born."

Brenda reached out to place a consoling hand on his knee. "Look, Summer has made it clear she doesn't want you there," she said bluntly.

"That doesn't mean I won't be."

Again, his mother and oldest sister exchanged glances, which annoyed him. It obviously had something to do with pitying him or with women things he couldn't be expected to understand, or maybe both.

"Brett," Brenda began again, "if she doesn't want you there, she may not even call you when it's time."

Hmm, he thought, that was probably true, although it had never occurred to him before. Just like that damn doctor's appointment. She hadn't wanted him there, so she'd made sure he *wasn't* there.

"And as much as I hate to say this, dear," his mother added, "if she really doesn't want you there, it'll be hard. Not just for the baby's birth, either. Afterward, too."

"So what you're saying is...?"

His mother sighed. "If you're worried about missing the baby's first months, being here or being in Paris won't make much of a difference. You have certain rights as the father, but that probably won't include seeing the baby every single day."

"I could file for joint custody," he said, feeling defensive.

His mother frowned. "I know you're going through a

difficult time right now, Brett, and I'm sure you're angry at Summer, but I know you care for her."

"And...?" Why wouldn't she just say what she meant?

"And I'm sure you don't want to hurt her that way, or hurt the baby, by battling over it, shuffling it back and forth all the time."

He couldn't believe he was having this conversation. "So you're suggesting I forget the baby, give it up?"

"No, of course not," his mother reassured him with a pronounced shake of her head. "I'm suggesting that you go to Paris, come back for a week when the baby is born, then make arrangements to come back for a few days every month or so until the assignment is over."

"Sure, you could stay here, fight over custody, drag the baby back and forth a couple of times each week, all that," Brenda chimed in, "but face it, Brett. That really wouldn't be good for anybody. Least of all the child."

Brett sighed and ran his hands back through his hair. He hated to admit it, but they made sense. Maybe getting away would be good. Maybe some time apart would make Summer come to her senses. If not, maybe it would at least make her feel secure enough with the baby that she wouldn't mind sharing custody with him when he returned, or at least giving him generous visitation.

Visitation. The word itself irritated him. This wasn't how it was supposed to be. But it's how things *were* and he had to deal with it.

Even so, he found himself flashing an angry glance at his sister. "Seems like this is what you wanted for me all along, isn't it?"

Brenda gave him a long, hard look—hesitant, and maybe a little guilty. "I just want what's best for you, Brett. And I believe that things happen for a reason and that fate has a way of working things out the right way. You convinced me before that things wouldn't have turned out like they had if you weren't meant to marry Summer. Now...well, I guess I'm thinking the same thing, just in reverse. If she doesn't want to marry you, maybe this is fate's way of telling you to go to Paris."

He released a long sigh. He'd had some of these same thoughts not long ago, only it had been easier to swallow when "fate" had made Summer love him and want to share her life with him. Having "fate" shut him out and take away what was most important to him was a lot more difficult to accept.

"She doesn't have any family, you know," he reminded them. "What if she needs somebody? Like when it comes time to have the baby, what if she needs me? Or what if she needs somebody afterward?"

"Who's her labor coach?" his mother asked.

Now that it wasn't him, he didn't even know. How sad was that? "I'm not sure. Maybe Tina."

"Well then," his mother said, "she'll have Tina. And on Saturday, when Susan and I go get your things, we'll talk with Summer. We'll tell her that if she needs us for anything, anything at all, we'll be here for her. You don't have to worry about her being alone, son," she added, patting his knee.

One last question still lingered in Brett's mind, though. One stupid question that he already knew the answer to.

What if she changes her mind? What if she decides she loves me and I'm not here?

Yet he knew that wouldn't happen. Couldn't happen. *I don't love you.* The words still rang in his ears and scalded his heart. They'd drained every ounce of hope for happiness that had still existed inside him. She didn't love him, and she wanted to have her baby alone.

As if to add to his thoughts, Brenda gave him a sympathetic look and said, "I know this is probably hard for you to believe, but if she doesn't want to marry you, Brett, you're better off this way. It's just a blessing that it happened now."

Now. That word, too, stuck in his brain. Maybe his mother and sister were right. Maybe this had happened *now* because somebody somewhere was telling him to go to Paris. Maybe that's why Bruseaux had called today. Maybe going to Paris would truly be the best thing Brett could do.

Not that his heart was really in the project anymore—he'd practically forgotten about it. But maybe he should go, anyway. Maybe it would be the best thing for everybody.

BRETT SAT ON THE FRONT porch of his parents' house in the middle of the night, a can of beer in one hand. He couldn't sleep. His boyhood room had once been a private sanctuary, and a vast luxury—his sisters had had to share a room, and he'd gotten his own, since he was the only boy—but suddenly it seemed like a tiny, stifling place to Brett. He didn't belong here anymore.

One part of him still thought he belonged at Summer's house, with her. Another part of him continued to question if maybe everyone was right, and maybe he belonged in Paris right now. The only thing he knew with any certainty was that he belonged somewhere other than where he was. He stood at a major crossroad in his life and he had to choose a direction very soon.

He leaned back in the porch chair and studied the shadows cast by the streetlights. He looked at them until they began to blur completely. Closing his eyes, he saw some of the sketches and other ideas he'd sent to Bruseaux, sketches for the glass megatower. He saw the same sharp lines and curving arcs he'd put on paper—lines and arcs that had made his blood race with satisfaction and excitement. He'd known they were good, and it had made him proud.

His mind drifted then to the interviews with Bruseaux, to the intuitive feeling Brett had had. He'd never told anyone, had barely even admitted it to himself, yet somehow he'd known almost before the phone call had come that he'd be the one Bruseaux would choose to design the building with him.

At the time, it had been everything to Brett. He'd slept with Summer by then already, and been abandoned by her already, too. He'd thought she was a closed chapter in his life and, although he'd been disappointed, he'd let the Paris job cheer him up and remind him that the world beckoned, that it was time to move on.

Now, strangely, as he'd realized earlier, the project meant little to him. When he imagined sitting in some lavish studio working side by side with Andre Bruseaux, instead of feeling the same excitement he'd once anticipated, he feared he'd feel...empty. Lonely. As if he was someplace he shouldn't be, even someplace where nothing was happening. He feared he'd sit and think of Summer all day, and of their baby. That, he thought, would be where something *important* was happening, and if he was in Paris, he'd miss it all.

"Aw, damn it," he muttered in the darkness.

Because again, the ugly truth came back to hit him in the face. This wasn't a choice he was making; Summer had already made the choice *for* him. Even if "with her" was where all the important stuff was happening, she still didn't want him there.

He'd tried every damn way he knew to try, but Summer had simply worn him down. She'd made him too tired to fight anymore, and what his mother and Brenda had told him today suddenly seemed real, and true, and like the only right answer. If Summer insisted on shutting him out of her life, the only sensible move was to go to Paris. Wasn't it?

"You win, Summer," he muttered into the darkness of the summer night. "You finally win."

"ALL RIGHT," Brett said into the phone. "I'll be arriving in Paris on August twentieth, Mr. Bruseaux." Then he hung up.

Well, that was it. The travel plans were made. His furniture was being transferred from his parents' garage into a storage facility, Anna was being assigned other duties until his return late next year and he was leaving Summer.

Despite all the guideposts he'd thought he'd recognized, the decision had been filled with a lot of angst and heartache. Still, his family had convinced him that leaving didn't mean leaving the baby, and he'd decided to believe them, to believe there would be plenty of time for the baby down the road.

Still, leaving Cincinnati felt like leaving Summer. *Really* leaving her. He knew she didn't want him around, yet it was still hard to completely give up on the woman he'd fallen in love with. He recalled that day just over a week ago when he'd held her so tenderly and listened to her breathing and felt such love for her. It was just a memory now, although it made his heart feel as if it was cracking.

He kept being tempted to call her, to try to change her mind one last time, but slowly, surely and painfully her words from that last day had begun to sink in. She didn't love him, and there was no coming back from that.

In his heart, he still felt he was meant to be with her, that they were meant to make a family together. But her heart clearly told her something different, so what else was there for him to do but go to Paris and try to get on with his life? It wasn't what he wanted to do, but it seemed the only move Summer had left him.

9

SUMMER REREAD the article she'd been reading all day. She knew, of course, that her plan had worked and Brett was going to Paris—his mother and Susan had filled her in when they'd come to pick up his things—yet seeing the words before her made it real.

Not just that he was going to Paris, but that he was going on, having a life without her. She suddenly felt surprisingly hurt that he could move on from what they'd shared, yet what choice had she given him? And that *had* been the whole idea, hadn't it?

So, she thought, still studying the paper, she'd given Brett's story to the real Mary Peterson. She bit her lip, looking at the black-and-white picture of him and his boss that accompanied it. Even in dull grayish ink, Brett looked...sad. His eyes seemed wilted.

She was probably just imagining it, though. He was going off to pursue his dream, after all. What did he have to be sad about?

Tired of feeling sad herself, Summer closed the business section and set the paper aside, then headed upstairs to start sorting through some of the things she'd gotten at a baby shower her co-workers had thrown at the office last week. She'd also bought a toy box and a changing table, both of which had been delivered just yesterday, so maybe she could start filling the toy box or hanging some of the tiny clothes she'd received in the closet.

When she stepped inside the nursery, though, the cheerful walls depressed her. They still reminded her of Brett. As she sat in her new rocking chair fiddling with baby toys and sleeper sets and miniature sweatsuits and blue jeans, she wished he were there sorting through it all with her. She could practically see his eyes light up at the sight of the tiny yellow socks she held between her fingers.

A glance at the new baby bed only added to her gloom. She liked the one they'd borrowed from Jackie better, and she wanted it back. She wanted them *all* back, the whole Ford family. And she wanted *him* back, too.

She still couldn't believe she'd gone through with throwing him out. How had she managed that? How had she actually succeeded in telling him she didn't love him? It broke her heart just remembering. After almost a month without him, she knew if he walked through that door right now, she'd throw herself into his arms and promise to love him forever.

Summer released a deep sigh, then tried to get up from the rocking chair. Oh drat, she couldn't pull herself up! If she couldn't get out of a simple rocking chair *now*, how the heck would she do it a month or two more down the road? For a brief second, she wanted to cry, because she couldn't help thinking that if Brett were here, she wouldn't be having this problem. He'd be taking her hands, pulling her to her feet, smiling and telling her that this was just another part of expecting a baby, and that before she knew it, she'd get her reward. But instead she was by herself, trapped in this chair, rocking it haphazardly back and forth in the hopes of getting up enough momentum to get to her feet.

After maneuvering her way out of the chair, Summer descended the stairs and found the newspaper again, opening it back up to Brett's picture.

She studied his eyes once more, remembering how blue they were, and how warm they shone when he was being sweet, or playful, or romantic, or most anytime at all.

So maybe she wasn't imagining it. Maybe he really *did* look sad.

Oh God, what if she'd actually been wrong about all this? What if marrying her and being with the baby *wasn't* holding him back from Paris? What if she'd truly been his choice?

She'd never thought about that before, that he might actually choose her and the baby over his career, but she knew that given the same choice right now—fashion design school or Brett—she'd make a decision she'd have never believed possible. She'd choose *him*. Hands down.

Her heart pumped wildly and her stomach began to churn. Could it really be? Could he really have wanted her more than that job all along?

She released the breath she hadn't realized she'd been holding and thought, *What do I do now?*

Well, for one thing, she should find out when he was leaving. She returned to the paper and scanned the text. Late August, it said, was when he would depart. And today was the twentieth, so late August was *now*. Without delay, she went to the phone and dialed Susan's number.

"Susan," she said when Brett's sister answered, "it's Summer."

"Oh, Summer, hi," she said, clearly surprised. "Is anything wrong?"

"No, everything's fine," Summer replied, then steeled

her courage. "Susan, I was wondering...when is Brett leaving for Paris?"

Susan hesitated. "Why?"

Summer took a deep breath and decided, *What the hell, why not just be honest?* "Because I've just realized that I've made a horrible mistake," she admitted. "I love him."

"Oh God," Susan said, sounding frantic.

"Oh God what?"

"Oh God, his plane leaves in less than an hour, Summer! Mom just took him to the airport!"

"Oh God!" Summer said.

"Listen, I'll drop everything and be over to pick you up!"

"No," Summer told her. "That'll take too long. I can get there faster myself."

"But, Summer—"

"No time, Susan. Gotta go. Bye."

Summer hung up the phone, found her keys and ran out the door. She squeezed behind the wheel of her car and took off for the airport.

She tried to drive at a reasonable speed, but it was difficult to keep her foot from pressing down harder on the gas pedal. She had less than an hour and the airport was more than half an hour away in good traffic.

She had to get to Brett before he left, she just had to! She had to tell him she really *did* love him, from the bottom of her heart! Even if he still chose to go, she couldn't let him leave without letting him know!

Thirty-five minutes after speaking with Susan, Summer pulled up at the passenger drop-off area at the airport and threw her car into Park. She abandoned the car and rushed through the wide revolving door, not caring if she got a parking ticket. She only wished she knew how much time she had left!

She quickly found the departure board and scanned the endless lines of flight information until she saw it—Flight 452 to Paris, Gate B12, leaving at 7:30 p.m. Summer checked her watch. It was 7:22, and getting to Concourse B required a walk and a tram ride and another walk.

After practically jogging down an enormous escalator, Summer ran as fast as she could to the security checkpoint, threw her purse on the conveyor belt and hurried through the metal-detector archway. Thank God, nothing beeped! She was often stopped for things like belt buckles and metal shoe decorations, but today she was wearing a sweatsuit and had never been happier to be casually dressed!

She bolted toward the subway-like tram, her heart beating a mile a minute as she waited for it. When finally it arrived, she stepped on board and grabbed on to one of the hanging straps overhead. A man tried to give her his seat, one of only a few built into the tram, but she refused, feeling far too panicky to sit.

The ride seemed interminably long, and when she checked her watch, it was 7:29! "Come on, come on," she muttered through clenched teeth, exasperated.

When she finally exited at Concourse B, she found herself at Gate B1. Oh no, that meant she had to get past eleven gates in about a minute!

All she could do was run.

She avoided the moving walkways, afraid they'd slow her down, and kept to the carpeted floor. She sprinted as quickly as her six months of pregnancy would allow, and watched the gate numbers move slowly past her. B3...B4...B5.

She checked her watch as she ran. Oh, damn! It was 7:33! *Please let them be running late! Please!*

Around B9 her belly began to feel heavy and her legs weak. But then B12 came into sight in the distance like an oasis in a desert. Just a little farther now! She could make it! *She had to!*

She moved into the waiting area at Gate B12, breathless. But, to Summer's horror, the flight attendant was shutting the door that led to the plane!

"Wait," Summer half yelled, half panted. "Please wait!" she managed to shout.

The flight attendant looked up, obviously taken aback by the sight of the exhausted pregnant woman before her. "What can I do for you, ma'am? Are you all right?"

"I have to get on that plane," Summer breathed, reaching the door.

The flight attendant smiled. "Well, I'll just need to see your boarding pass and—"

Summer had no energy to argue about a boarding pass that she didn't have, and she wasn't exactly trying to stow away, either, so she did the only thing that made sense in the moment. Using her last ounce of energy, she pushed past the woman and walked quickly through the doorway and down the long narrow hall that led onto the plane.

"Hey, wait! You can't get on the plane without a boarding pass!" the flight attendant yelled behind her. Then she gave chase, forcing Summer back into a run. She had to reach Brett before it was too late!

She burst onto the plane, which was filled to capacity. All eyes were on her—the crazed pregnant woman who had just leaped on the plane like she was some superhero coming to someone's rescue. Following right behind her came the flight attendant.

"Brett!" Summer yelled.

"Oh my God," she heard him say from somewhere. She saw him then, about eight rows back, next to the window. He stared at her openmouthed, looking completely aghast. "What are you doing here?"

"I came to tell you—"

"You have to get off the plane," the flight attendant said, grabbing her wrist.

"But—" She'd been about to tell him that she loved him, right in front of all these people and everything, only to have the flight attendant stop her. She couldn't believe it. This was too cruel to be true! "Let go of me!"

"Hey, that's my fiancée," Brett said, rising from his seat.

"She doesn't have a boarding pass," the flight attendant snapped.

"But I just came to tell you—"

"You have to get off the plane! Now!"

Summer shook her arm free from the flight attendant and saw that Brett was climbing over the man next to him, tripping actually, trying to get to the aisle as he said, "What did you come to tell me, Summer?"

"I came to tell you that I love you, and that I want to marry you, and that I was a fool to ever shove you out of my life."

Brett caught his breath and clamped his hands on the tops of the seats on either side of him for balance. She loved him? His heart felt like it might burst in his chest. "But I thought...you didn't."

"I lied," she blurted out. "I loved you all along, and I want you with me. Forever."

Brett couldn't have been happier. Or more baffled. This made no sense. And this probably wasn't the best time to discuss it, considering that an airplane full of people were gaping at their entire exchange, not to mention the angry flight attendant who stood behind Summer, scowling, yet... "What about your independence? I thought you had to be in control of everything in your life?"

"I discovered," she said, "that I'd rather be *out* of control, if it's with you."

A laugh of pure joy escaped Brett's throat, but then he remembered.... "Summer, if you've loved me all along, then...why did all this bad stuff happen?"

"Brenda told me about your job in Paris," she said. "I didn't want to ruin your dreams, Brett."

Brett's heart flooded with an emotion he couldn't name. He could barely fathom what she'd just told him. He'd remember to kill his sister later for not mentioning this to him, but in the meantime... Summer had dumped him because of Paris? Because she thought he'd rather go to Paris than be with her and their child? It seemed unbelievable that she could think that...until he remembered her own lost dreams, and the very reason she'd not wanted to marry him in the first place.

"I didn't want to hold you back," she added. "I wanted you to have everything you wanted."

"Summer," he said, "don't you know? *You're* what I want. Since the day I met you, you've been what I want."

"What about Paris? What about the job?"

"Paris is nothing compared to you. It never was. I couldn't be happier anywhere in the world than I could be here, with you and our baby."

Summer was warmed by his wonderful words, but filled with remorse over all the trouble she'd caused between them, too. "I'm sorry I wasn't honest with you, Brett! I'm so sorry for everything!"

"No," he said, finally reaching her and lifting a finger to her lips. "I wasn't honest, either. I didn't tell you about the job because I didn't want to give you another reason to turn me down. But the way I see it, we love each other, and soon we're gonna have a baby to love *together*. Does anything else matter?"

Summer thought about all the things she had let stand between them for so long. Her control, her job, his obligations, his opportunities. And he was right. None of it mattered, not anymore. "No," she said, shaking her head. "Nothing matters but us."

THE DULCET STRAINS of the harp filled the air, each note like a tiny silver drop of rain that fell over Summer and helped to calm her. Yet who could be calm? She was about to walk up an aisle between two hundred people, many of whom she didn't know, and marry the man of her dreams.

"You can do this," she whispered to her reflection in the floor-length mirror in the church's dressing room. Then she studied the picture she saw before her in the glass.

The dress remained as lovely as she remembered, and no longer made her feel silly or girlish. As Jackie had said that day in the bridal salon, it was simple yet elegant, even in pregnancy. Summer's hair was swept off her neck in a loose French twist, soft tendrils curving down over her cheeks and neck, and a veil of tulle cascaded down her back.

A short strand of pearls, old, and borrowed from Brett's mother, graced her throat. In one gloved hand Summer clutched a small bouquet of short-stemmed yellow roses, and in the other the embroidered handkerchief displaying a restitched date and qualifying as new.

Pinned to it was a tiny blue ribbon saved by Mrs. Ford from Brett's birth.

"You can do this," she told herself again.

Then Tina approached behind her in her bridesmaid's dress, squeezing her hand and saying, "It's time. Good luck!"

A moment later, the harpist took up a new melody, which Summer recognized as the one she'd chosen to walk down the aisle to, and as if by magic, her jitters vanished. This was the moment she'd been working toward with Brett since the night she'd met him, the culmination of all their combined dreams. She couldn't wait to be his wife!

A rush of pure joy raced through Summer's body as she strolled down the aisle. Smiling eyes fell upon her from all directions, but all she could see was Brett at the end, waiting for her, looking handsome and happy and perfect.

She tried to slow her progress, tried to walk in step with the soft, elegant music, but she just wanted to get to him. She wanted to take her vows and promise herself to him forever.

When she reached Brett and his warm, blue gaze fell on her, she'd never felt so beautiful in her life, and when he took her hand and turned with her to face the minister, her entire world felt...grand. She spoke her vows boldly, with pride, and she smiled at Brett as she said them.

"Brett, you may kiss your bride."

His mouth pressing against hers was like a thousand symphonies. She wrapped her arms around his neck, and when he began to end the kiss, she drew him back for more, getting lost in the way she wanted him.

"Ladies and gentleman," the minister said, "may I present to you Mr. and Mrs. Brett Ford."

"I love you," she whispered to him beneath the applause of the congregation.

"I love you, too, Mrs. Ford," he replied with his classic crooked grin.

And Summer knew, now that she'd finally pushed everything else out of the way, that real life, real living, could begin, with her child, and with her husband, who had opened her heart to love.

_____Epilogue_____

SUMMER SET HER SKETCH PAD aside to answer the phone. "Hello?"

"Hi, babe." She smiled at the sound of Brett's voice. A year later, she remained just as entranced by him as she'd ever been. "How's Amy?"

Summer glanced at the baby sleeping in the bassinet nearby. "Quieter, now. I think she just missed her daddy earlier." She'd been fussy when Brett had called home at lunchtime.

His voice took on a playful tone as he said, "And how's my _other_ girl?"

"Busy," Summer replied. "I've got a ton of work to do before class on Monday."

"I'll tell you what," he said. "When I get home, we can grab a quick dinner out, then I'll entertain Amy while you work. Sound good?"

"Sounds great," Summer told him.

Hanging up the phone a minute later, she glanced once more at her sleeping daughter, remembering a conversation she'd shared with Brett after Amy's birth.

"You aren't disappointed?" she'd asked, peering up at him from the hospital bed, the new baby asleep in her arms.

"Disappointed?" Brett had replied.

"She's not a boy."

A tender smile had grown on his handsome face.

"How could I possibly be disappointed? She's perfect and beautiful, just like her mother."

Summer retrieved her pad and pencil and got back to work, sketching a sleek evening gown. But then she stopped once more and shifted her gaze toward the window, where she could see the Eiffel Tower in the distance. She couldn't believe this was her life—this man, this child, this city. It all still seemed too good to be true.

Summer had never even thought about the possibility of going to design school, but Brett had suggested it soon after they'd brought Amy home from the hospital, pointing out that her income wasn't as vital now that they were married. It hadn't been easy giving up her hard-won position at Stafford's, but when the dream had once again become possibility—and when she'd actually been accepted to a school in Paris!—there'd been no question of what to do.

In another year she would graduate, and Andre Bruseaux was more than happy to keep Brett busy until then. After that, they would bring Amy home to the States, where Brett would continue his career and Summer would attempt to start a new one, one that she already loved from the bottom of her heart.

A year ago, she'd learned that sometimes making sacrifices were worth it for someone you loved. Now she'd learned that sometimes it could open the door to all your dreams.

Every mother wants to see her children marry
and have little ones of their own.

One mother decided to take matters into
her own hands....

Now three Texas-born brothers are about to discover
that mother knows best: A strong man *does* need a
good woman. And babies make a forever family!

Matters of the Heart

A Mother's Day collection of
three **brand-new** stories by

Pamela Morsi
Ann Major
Annette Broadrick

Available in April at your favorite retail outlets,
only from Silhouette Books!

Where love comes alive™

Harlequin truly does make any time special. . . . This year we are celebrating weddings in style!

A Walk Down the Aisle

WEDDING CELEBRATION

To help us celebrate, we want you to tell us how wearing the Harlequin wedding gown will make your wedding day special. As the grand prize, Harlequin will offer one lucky bride the chance to **"Walk Down the Aisle"** in the Harlequin wedding gown!

There's more...

For her honeymoon, she and her groom will spend five nights at the **Hyatt Regency Maui.** As part of this five-night honeymoon at the hotel renowned for its romantic attractions, the couple will enjoy a candlelit dinner for two in Swan Court, a sunset sail on the hotel's catamaran, and duet spa treatments.

A HYATT RESORT AND SPA ®

MAUI
the Magic Isles™

Maui • Molokai • Lanai

To enter, please write, in, 250 words or less, how wearing the Harlequin wedding gown will make your wedding day special. The entry will be judged based on its emotionally compelling nature, its originality and creativity, and its sincerity. This contest is open to Canadian and U.S. residents only and to those who are 18 years of age and older. There is no purchase necessary to enter. Void where prohibited. See further contest rules attached. Please send your entry to:

Walk Down the Aisle Contest

In Canada	In U.S.A.
P.O. Box 637	P.O. Box 9076
Fort Erie, Ontario	3010 Walden Ave.
L2A 5X3	Buffalo, NY 14269-9076

You can also enter by visiting www.eHarlequin.com

Win the Harlequin wedding gown and the vacation of a lifetime!
The deadline for entries is October 1, 2001.

HARLEQUIN®
Makes any time special ®

PHWDACONT1

HARLEQUIN WALK DOWN THE AISLE TO MAUI CONTEST 1197
OFFICIAL RULES
NO PURCHASE NECESSARY TO ENTER

1. To enter, follow directions published in the offer to which you are responding. Contest begins April 2, 2001, and ends on October 1, 2001. Method of entry may vary. Mailed entries must be postmarked by October 1, 2001, and received by October 8, 2001.

2. Contest entry may be, at times, presented via the Internet, but will be restricted solely to residents of certain geographic areas that are disclosed on the Web site. To enter via the Internet, if permissible, access the Harlequin Web site (www.eHarlequin.com) and follow the directions displayed online. Online entries must be received by 11:59 p.m. E.S.T. on October 1, 2001.

   In lieu of submitting an entry online, enter by mail by hand-printing (or typing) on an 8½" x 11" plain piece of paper, your name, address (including zip code), Contest number/name and in 250 words or fewer, why winning a Harlequin wedding dress would make your wedding day special. Mail via first-class mail to: Harlequin Walk Down the Aisle Contest 1197, (in the U.S.) P.O. Box 9076, 3010 Walden Avenue, Buffalo, NY 14269-9076, (in Canada) P.O. Box 637, Fort Erie, Ontario L2A 5X3, Canada.

   Limit one entry per person, household address and e-mail address. Online and/or mailed entries received from persons residing in geographic areas in which Internet entry is not permissible will be disqualified.

3. Contests will be judged by a panel of members of the Harlequin editorial, marketing and public relations staff based on the following criteria:
   - Originality and Creativity—50%
   - Emotionally Compelling—25%
   - Sincerity—25%

   In the event of a tie, duplicate prizes will be awarded. Decisions of the judges are final.

4. All entries become the property of Torstar Corp. and will not be returned. No responsibility is assumed for lost, late, illegible, incomplete, inaccurate, nondelivered or misdirected mail or misdirected e-mail, for technical, hardware or software failures of any kind, lost or unavailable network connections, or failed, incomplete, garbled or delayed computer transmission or any human error which may occur in the receipt or processing of the entries in this Contest.

5. Contest open only to residents of the U.S. (except Puerto Rico) and Canada, who are 18 years of age or older, and is void wherever prohibited by law; all applicable laws and regulations apply. Any litigation within the Province of Quebec respecting the conduct or organization of a publicity contest may be submitted to the Régie des alcools, des courses et des jeux for a ruling. Any litigation respecting the awarding of a prize may be submitted to the Régie des alcools, des courses et des jeux only for the purpose of helping the parties reach a settlement. Employees and immediate family members of Torstar Corp. and D. L. Blair, Inc., their affiliates, subsidiaries and all other agencies, entities and persons connected with the use, marketing or conduct of this Contest are not eligible to enter. Taxes on prizes are the sole responsibility of winners. Acceptance of any prize offered constitutes permission to use winner's name, photograph or other likeness for the purposes of advertising, trade and promotion on behalf of Torstar Corp., its affiliates and subsidiaries without further compensation to the winner, unless prohibited by law.

6. Winners will be determined no later than November 15, 2001, and will be notified by mail. Winners will be required to sign and return an Affidavit of Eligibility form within 15 days after winner notification. Noncompliance within that time period may result in disqualification and an alternative winner may be selected. Winners of trip must execute a Release of Liability prior to ticketing and must possess required travel documents (e.g. passport, photo ID) where applicable. Trip must be completed by November 2002. No substitution of prize permitted by winner. Torstar Corp. and D. L. Blair, Inc., their parents, affiliates, and subsidiaries are not responsible for errors in printing or electronic presentation of Contest, entries and/or game pieces. In the event of printing or other errors which may result in unintended prize values or duplication of prizes, all affected game pieces or entries shall be null and void. If for any reason the Internet portion of the Contest is not capable of running as planned, including infection by computer virus, bugs, tampering, unauthorized intervention, fraud, technical failures, or any other causes beyond the control of Torstar Corp. which corrupt or affect the administration, secrecy, fairness, integrity or proper conduct of the Contest, Torstar Corp. reserves the right, at its sole discretion, to disqualify any individual who tampers with the entry process and to cancel, terminate, modify or suspend the Contest or the Internet portion thereof. In the event of a dispute regarding an online entry, the entry will be deemed submitted by the authorized holder of the e-mail account submitted at the time of entry. Authorized account holder is defined as the natural person who is assigned to an e-mail address by an Internet access provider, online service provider or other organization that is responsible for arranging e-mail address for the domain associated with the submitted e-mail address. **Purchase or acceptance of a product offer does not improve your chances of winning.**

7. Prizes: (1) Grand Prize—A Harlequin wedding dress (approximate retail value: $3,500) and a 5-night/6-day honeymoon trip to Maui, HI, including round-trip air transportation provided by Maui Visitors Bureau from Los Angeles International Airport (winner is responsible for transportation to and from Los Angeles International Airport) and a Harlequin Romance Package, including hotel accomodations (double occupancy) at the Hyatt Regency Maui Resort and Spa, dinner for (2) two at Swan Court, a sunset sail on Kiele V and a spa treatment for the winner (approximate retail value: $4,000); (5) Five runner-up prizes of a $1000 gift certificate to selected retail outlets to be determined by Sponsor (retail value $1000 ea.). Prizes consist of only those items listed as part of the prize. Limit one prize per person. All prizes are valued in U.S. currency.

8. For a list of winners (available after December 17, 2001) send a self-addressed, stamped envelope to: Harlequin Walk Down the Aisle Contest 1197 Winners, P.O. Box 4200 Blair, NE 68009-4200 or you may access the www.eHarlequin.com Web site through January 15, 2002.

Contest sponsored by Torstar Corp., P.O. Box 9042, Buffalo, NY 14269-9042, U.S.A.

PHWDACONT2

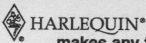